Enlightenment:
Oathkeeper

Enlightenment: Oathkeeper

Derek Hitchmough

Library of Congress Control Number:		2013920349
ISBN:	Hardcover	978-1-4931-2680-4
	Softcover	978-1-4931-2679-8
	eBook	978-1-4931-2681-1

This book was printed in the United States of America.

Rev. date: 11/15/2013

To order additional copies of this book, contact:
Xlibris LLC
1-888-795-4274
www.Xlibris.com
Orders@Xlibris.com
141727

CONTENTS

To Yasmin
who's helped so much with this series.

A City in Chaos

June 30, 2027

The city was burning. Fires burned out of control everywhere, pillars of thick black smoke rising. Lightning struck all around, the sky dark with unnatural thunderclouds. Fireballs materialized out of nowhere, raining down on the city, adding to the blaze. Ice and wind tornadoes sprouted from within the city itself, only adding to the pandemonium.

"My god . . . what happened?"

Keith's whisper was a mix of horror and devastation, all that and more reflected in his amber-brown eyes. He stood stock-still, his brown hair lightly moving in the evening breeze. Next to him, the three teenagers were in much the same state. Veren was the first to recover, growing fiercely determined.

"We have to help! The city's in trouble!" he shouted, which jolted the others out of their shock. Keith quickly nodded and ran off, rallying the other students and adults to help.

While he was doing so, Bri quickly turned to her friends. "What are we gonna do, Veren?" she asked, her pulse pounding.

"Well, that's obvious, Bri. We go out there and help!" said Veren, brushing his bangs out of his blue eyes. "However we can"

Emmy glanced at him, holding out her right hand. "And punish those responsible" she whispered, her warpblade appearing with a flash of light in her hand.

After a moment, Veren nodded. "Right," he said, then addressed both of them. "Okay, we'll split up and go across the rooftops. Help whoever you can and do what you can to stop whoever's responsible, but don't get yourselves hurt".

They both nodded, though Veren grimaced slightly as he said *rooftops*. Without further ado, all three of them ran toward the school gates, and within minutes they had wall-climbed up to the rooftops.

Brianna stopped on her rooftop, staring out at her improved view of the destruction for a moment. Shaking her head, she got a running start and leapt from building to building, heading toward a big building, half of which was on fire.

Soon she arrived, nimbly landing on the ground and quickly assessing the damage. She tried the front door, but it wouldn't open. Grunting, she kicked the door several times, with no visible results. Backing up, she ran toward it with a yell, but all this got was a bruise on her shoulder.

She grunted slightly, massaging the spot for a moment. "Gotta do this the hard way" she muttered to herself, her left hand glowing yellow.

Aiming her hand, she sent lightning bolts at the door.

The door caved in with a bang, a bunch of rubble shoved out of the way.

She quickly ducked inside; flames were everywhere, the crackling overpowering every other sound. It was getting hard to breathe without coughing, and she was sweating profusely. She quickly ran up a flight of stairs, noting they were crumbling and in danger of collapsing already. She had to hurry.

Within minutes, she had located all the people still trapped within the building. One of the children—who was heavier than she looked—was slung over her shoulder. Using her warpblade, she teleported them all outside and away from the building.

Now outside, Brianna sighed in relief, slowly putting down the little girl. Still holding her warpblade, she looked them over quickly. They were all wounded, mostly from small burns, and still in terrified shock.

"Okay" she breathed, then blinked hard; some of the smoke was still in her eyes. "Go to Keith's school. You'll get healing there, and you'll be safe" she said quickly, pointing her warpblade toward the school. "That way"

Maybe it was the fact that she'd saved their lives, but they managed to flee where she directed. The little girl remained though, clearly on the verge of crying.

"Please" Brianna whispered, feeling a bit unsure of what to say. "Go with them, you'll be okay"

"I'm scared" she whimpered, and the tears fell. "My parents . . . They couldn't . . ."

She couldn't go on; she bawled right then and there.

Brianna felt as if her heart had been stabbed, and she stared at the little girl. This was almost exactly like what had happened to her: she was very young, her entire world had been uprooted in an instant, including her parents.

Tears fell before she realized they were there, and her warp-blade clattered to the ground, lying several feet away, but she didn't care. She picked up the girl, holding her tightly.

"You'll be okay" she rasped, shaking a bit herself. "I swear it"

Crack! Crack!

Brianna turned around, then stared in horror. The burning building was collapsing, part of it cracking and falling toward *them*. By instinct, she tried to teleport out of the way.

But her warp-blade lay on the ground, far out of her reach, and she realized this a second too late; they were trapped.

There was a *swoosh*, a long drawn-out shred of wood, and a number of cracks as the building landed in pieces on the ground.

After several seconds, Brianna slowly opened her eyes, completely surprised to find that one, they were alive, and two, the building was now in several pieces on either side of her. In addition, they were relatively unscathed, except for a thick coating of dust and small debris.

The large pieces of the building had been cut clean through, with almost perfectly straight lines. Along those edges, a glowing purple-black magic flickered briefly.

Brianna slowly brought her attention toward it's source, and her heart leapt at the sight.

The creature before her was an eleven-foot-tall Fenrir—a rather monstrous species of wolves—with dark-blue fur and black stripes. He stood in a crouching position, his right paw outstretched and his six-inch long claws glowing a purple-black, the same as the building's edges had been.

With a slight growl, the Fenrir slowly turned in the cramped space and faced her, his yellow eyes looking at her instantly. His thin, lightning-shaped scar; the slightly flattened-down mane on his neck; and his standing-on-end tail fur were all instantly recognizable to her.

The little girl cried out in fear, clinging to her, but Brianna didn't notice.

With a smile, she quickly put the little girl on the ground and ran forward, hugging Fenrir's head. Fenrir growled in affection as he slowly lay down on his paws, rubbing his head against her touch. "Fenrir," she whispered softly against his fur, somewhat buried in it, "I missed you, big guy"

The little girl promptly fainted.

He growled again in affection. It was true: it had been about six months since she had last seen him. He had saved her life as well as her best friends at that time.

Boom!

The rumble that followed jolted both of them, quickly bringing Brianna back into reality. She stepped away from Fenrir, her expression growing serious. They would have time for a reunion later.

"All right, Fenrir, we have to do our best to help" she said, turning toward the source. Fenrir followed as best as he could due to the limited space, but they didn't get far.

Boom! Boom!

Both of them stopped at the twin explosions, which came from completely opposite directions. They looked at each other for a moment.

"Okay, change of plan," she said quickly. "You go that way, and get the ones responsible. I'll go back to Keith's school and drop off this little girl, then I'll come back to the other one. We'll meet back at the school in a few hours."

He nodded slightly, turning himself toward the source. Fenrir then made his way through the city as best as he could, with some difficulty through the smaller spaces.

Looking after him for a few seconds, she took a deep breath, then gathered up her warpblade. After that, she gently picked up the little girl, grunting slightly at her weight. *I can't believe my desire to help earlier made me forget this little girl, however briefly* she thought ruefully, sighing. *I'm so sorry.*

Still, she glanced up at the nearest rooftop.

A flash later, she reappeared at the top, then quickly jumped across the rooftops toward Keith's school. Jumping with the little girl's weight nearly made her miss the roof, and when she landed, she wobbled from the increased impact.

She let out a breath. Tonight was gonna be a *long* night.

Veren quickly landed on the top of his rooftop, then promptly got down on one knee clutching his stomach. He panted heavily, trying to calm down his innards, and most likely trying to turn his face less green.

He grunted. He *hated* walking up the sides of buildings. It always made his whole body churn, the way gravity suddenly turned sideways, but his stomach in particular took offense to it.

He shook his head hard then tried to stand; the situation demanded he get through this.

A minute later, he was jumping across the rooftops with practiced ease. And not seconds later, he heard a woman's scream . . . so naturally, he set off toward the source.

He quickly jumped off, landing with a grunt. The woman herself was in her thirties, a strawberry-blonde, but she was clutching her chest with both hands. Her breath was short and shallow and sounded similar to a hiss at times.

He was quickly at her side. "Are you okay, ma'am? I can help heal you" he said soothingly.

Maybe it was the warpblade he was holding, but she seemed reluctant. "I'd rather you didn't, actually" she said.

"This is a serious situation" he said with an edge; there was no time for this. "I have to at least look at the injury"

"Yeah? Well, the injured area is personal" she said with a huff, and with particular emphasis on *personal.*

He opened his mouth, then he remembered the way the woman had been clutching her chest when he'd arrived, and the particularly painful note she'd been breathing. Which meant that when she was clutching her chest, she was really clutching her-

Ohhhh . . . Right. Yeah he shouldn't go there. He didn't envy the healer who'd have to treat her.

He was sure his face was red, but he tried to ignore it: "Okay, fair point" he said, then pointed. "Instead, head to Keith's school. There'll be more experienced healers to deal with your injury. Can you walk?"

Short answer was, she could. But he did hear a grumbled comment about him, something about him having the nerve for trying to heal the afflicted area.

He was a little offended, but was willing to let it slide. And good thing too: not a second after the woman disappeared, a guard appeared on the scene.

Well, a former guard anyway. They had quit by launching this attack. This one in particular was male—as they all were—wore his armor, and had all-black eyes, except for the white bits. The eye color didn't surprise him, considering it was a sign of possession.

Despite the fact that this guard was merely one of the many lesser guards, it didn't stop Veren's hatred from rising. These possessed guards had messed with Bri since she'd come into this city, and that he couldn't forgive.

"Gonna stop me, kid?" the guard goaded with a smirk, briefly showing expression, which went right back to blank after it was done.

He chuckled, smiling without warmth. "Stop you?" Veren said. "Actually, I'm gonna tear you limb from limb!"

The guard didn't react; he just charged straight at him. Veren didn't even attempt to move backward.

Instead, he smirked and brought up a hand, which began to glow a light blue. The guard swung his sword at him, but Veren merely dodged the slash and slammed his hand onto the guard's chest. The guard grunted from the impact, but he quickly recovered and stabbed him—or he would have given the chance.

With his hand on the guard's chest, Veren coated him in rapidly growing ice. And the ice didn't stop at his chest; it kept going and going, leaving the guard struggling as he became buried under a thick coating of ice, until finally he was frozen solid in his attempted stabbing pose. Veren slowly removed his hand as he glared at the frozen guard, gripping his warp-blade.

He raised it, aiming to cut him limb from limb.

Halfway through the blow though, he stopped, his arms shaking. *No! I can't do that!* he thought, struggling against this darker side. *Not only is it crossing a line, it'd make me the same as them!*

Still, even with these thoughts, he knew he wanted this on some level; he darkly wanted revenge on them. And that frustrated him, having to deal with darkness tempting his every action.

He grit his teeth, straining against himself—then he slowly moved the warpblade away from the frozen guard. He would *not* allow himself to sink that low—not again.

He made a strangled growling sound, hating himself. Every time he got angry, or was in pain, darkness would physically inhabit his mind, tempting him down darker paths and actions. It took a lot of effort not to give in, but he knew he must fight it; otherwise he'd turn into a human-looking monster. If only there was something he could do about it!

An explosion nearby jarred him out of his thoughts, and he sighed, then ran off in it's direction.

Emmy dodged a sword slash, then easily slid her warp-blade down another guard's sword, and disarmed him. Then she hit him on the helmet with the hilt, hard.

She smirked, facing the last guard out of a group of eight fallen ones. "Come and get it," she snarled.

He charged with a battle-cry,—which didn't look well with the blank expression, not that she particularly cared—but she easily dodged every wild attack he made. And effortlessly blocked the attacks that would have connected, their battle filling the air with clangs.

She enjoyed toying with him, even as she saw another's face superimposed on this poor schmuck. The coal-black eyes, the similar hair color, that damning smirk of his: it angered her to no end.

Then she got bored, and easily shoved the guard to the ground. And just to make sure he blacked out, she slammed her warp-blade's hilt onto his helmet as well, enjoying the impact itself. Then she looked around at the eight fallen guards, her expression dark and her fists clenched. Then she opened her free hand, which began to glow yellow, and a low crackle filled the air.

She launched lightning from her palm, which broke off into eight separate tendrils, one latching onto each of the guards.

She smirked, watching as the lightning streaked through their nervous systems, shocking them repeatedly. They were just plain lucky they were already unconscious. *Let that be a lesson to those bastards* she thought grimly, only stopping after five seconds had passed, her mental endurance taking a small hit as an aftereffect. She would have prolonged it, but the situation demanded she not linger.

And as a prime indicator of that, screams filled the air as the other guards wreaked havoc on the city.

She looked up at the roof of the building to her right, then she disappeared with a flash. Now actually on the roof, she picked the direction of the loudest screams, and ran that way. It took her a minute to arrive at the source, but eventually she did.

Three guards had come across fleeing civilians.

Not on my watch she thought darkly, hand glowing light-blue this time. And immediately afterward, a sharp wall of ice drew itself between the guards and the civilians. Both were bewildered, especially since the wall she'd conjured was only about two feet tall.

"Get out of here!" she yelled down at them, startling both groups. "Now!"

The civilians came back to their senses and ran, leaving the guards to blankly stare up at her. She merely jumped off the roof, landing nimbly with practiced ease. Even before she landed, they got into a battle-ready position, their swords at the ready. She straightened slowly, glancing at their drawn swords, then smirked.

"Bring it on," she challenged.

A few hours later, it was just past midnight at Keith's school, and no one was sleeping. The school itself was overflowing with patients, and those who couldn't be treated inside were spread out in the courtyard. They were being treated as best as they could, but there were a lot of hurt people and only a few healers to go around, along with the limit to their healing magic.

Brianna sat on the school's front steps, doing her best to dust herself off, sighing numbly. She paused to brush the dust off the front of her shirt.

Nearby, Emmy was washing her long blond hair with magic, her green eyes hard but completely focused on the task. Veren was healing a number of cuts on himself, having already done the same for them. He nearly growled, then angrily brushed his bangs out of his vision.

"Those damn guards. When I get my hands on them, they're gonna pay" Veren muttered, working carefully on his back.

Beside him, Emmy snorted with derision, wringing her hair of excess water. "Get in line, Veren," she said, a fierce undercurrent of hatred in her voice. "If anyone's gonna get revenge, it's me"

They said nothing, but her two friends shuddered inside at her tone. Her hatred had been smoldering for nearly six months, and it made her act completely opposite from her normal personality. They knew they weren't the target of her hatred, but that didn't make it any easier. They just wanted the old Emmy back already.

"Yeah, those guards will pay dearly for this," Brianna nearly snarled, using magic to drip water onto her hair, which was coated with dust. There was a general muttered agreement from Emmy and Veren.

"Can't sleep?"

Brianna looked up to see Keith standing there beside them, his face drawn with grief and anger. Despite the tense situation, it made her feel better to see him again. "Hey there, Keith," she breathed, then she shook her head. "And no, I don't think we can"

He sighed, sitting down on the steps beside her. "I know what you mean. This is just terrible" he said, his eyes weak. He passed a hand over his eyes. Then he looked at her "But you should still get some sleep, Bri. Emmy and Veren, you too."

"Why?" Bri whispered, wringing her hair of water.

He smiled slightly, but only for a moment. "Well, because of . . . what happened, there's somewhere important I've gotta be tomorrow. And I'd like you three to come with me."

"Really?" Bri whispered, looking up at him, her hair still in her hands. "Where's that?"

But he wouldn't answer. Instead, he simply stood up and left, which made her stare after him. She felt even sadder as she did so.

"He's just as stressed as we are," Veren said, groaning slightly from his healing work, "quite likely more"

"Yeah" she agreed, looking after Keith. "But I don't like it at all"

Keith was the closest thing she had to a father figure now. She hated to see him like this.

Veren looked across the grounds, where the wounded that couldn't fit in the hospital wing laid out. "Those people, they didn't deserve this," he breathed, his tone growing angry. "Especially that little girl you found, Bri"

Bri looked down for a moment, not wanting Veren to see her cry again.

"By the way," he said, his voice lighter, "you did a good job calming her down"

"Did I?" she breathed, a bit surprised. She had been awkward and stumbling the whole time she tried, not having any clue how to comfort people, let alone a little girl. "I thought I did terrible."

A hand on her shoulder startled her, and she glanced behind her. "You did well, Bri," he said simply, a small smile on his face.

She slowly smiled a bit in return. "Thanks, Veren"

Emmy remained silent the entire time. Veren slowly glanced at her, that simple motion showing Bri he was just as aware of that as she was. He shared that same worry: what if Emmy never went back to normal?

ROYALTY

July 1, 2027

"What's taking Keith so long?" said Emmy, sounding bored as she leaned against the school wall.

Her two friends glanced at each other before looking at Emmy. Emmy straightened up with her arms crossed over her summer outfit, a light-red top and a thigh-length light-blue skirt.

"Well, when I passed him earlier, he seemed to be in a hurry," said Veren, rubbing his head slightly. "I tried to ask what was up, but he didn't answer me, other than telling us to put on something nice."

True to his statement, he was wearing his silver-gray T-shirt and dark-gold shorts instead of his normal training outfit. All over his shirt were realistic lightning strikes, often in midstrike.

"Good thing you told us about that part Veren, or we might have gotten yelled at or something," said Brianna. That was something she definitely didn't want happening. She wore her mid-sleeved dull-black shirt and dark-blue skirt, which went just past her thighs. On the front of her shirt was a large scale picture of Fenrir standing on a large shelf of rock with a full moon behind him.

Just then, the front doors of the school opened, and Keith strode out. All three friends blinked slightly, surprised by what they saw. While Keith wasn't wearing a business suit, what he was wearing was more formal than what he normally wore.

He looked over them with a smile as he walked, "Good, you're all up and ready," he said. Briefly walking past them, he asked, "Shall we get going?"

Looking at one another with surprised looks, they hurried after him. "If you don't mind my asking, where are we going?" Brianna asked, all three of them easily keeping pace. But Keith didn't answer her, which made her feel really odd.

The trip to their mysterious destination took a while, though as they walked, it became clearer and clearer that they were heading to the center of the city itself. As they walked though, they passed some of the attacked buildings, which were undergoing repair work. All four of them were grim as they walked past, still vividly remembering last night.

When Keith finally stopped, half-an-hour later, he stood there and slightly smiled up at the building ahead of them. "Well, this is our stop guys" he said, glancing back briefly with that smile.

All three teenagers, however, were staring in awe, completely overwhelmed.

The buildings before them weren't just fancy, they were outrageously luxurious. While the rest of the city wasn't too bad in looks, it was obvious that no expense had been spared for the centerpiece of the city. Even from what little they could see, it was obvious that the entire set of buildings spanned an entire mile or more. In addition, armored guards patrolled the perimeter, and most likely on the inside as well.

Keith took in a deep breath of the fresh air, smiling. "Ah. I can never get tired of looking at this sight" he said, chuckling a little to himself.

He then turned around, slowly raising an eyebrow at the still-stunned teenagers. Keith merely chuckled again gesturing toward the building. "You coming?" he asked, turning to walk forward again, which jolted them. With looks at one another, the three of them followed Keith toward the building's entrance.

On their path between the entrance and the door inside, Keith went through several layers of security with the teens trailing behind. It was a necessary evil, but time-consuming.

"Seriously, what's going on, Keith?" said Brianna, feeling slightly lost.

Keith glanced over his shoulder at her with a smile on his face. "You'll find out soon enough, sweetheart," he whispered gently, turning back around.

Brianna blinked, feeling a small wave of emotion running through her body. It made her feel strangely warm, but, why on earth had he just called her *sweetheart?*

There was a low whine in the air, then a subtle glow appeared out of nowhere, and a silver-gray symbol appeared directly on Keith's chest. Its slight glow attracted their attention.

While the three of them were startled by it's sudden appearance, Keith merely looked down at it as if he'd been expecting it. "Don't worry, this is just a helpful sign from the security that we passed. It tells everyone else that we're important and to be trusted," he said reassuringly. All the while, the glowing symbol on his chest continued to glow.

Brianna looked at her two friends, feeling something was seriously up. "Can someone help me?" she whispered.

"From the looks of it, we're here to visit someone important, and in person," Veren whispered back, though only after several seconds had passed. Both of them glanced at Emmy; this was more evidence that she wasn't being herself. "Maybe we'll get to see the royal family as well"

Brianna hummed slightly, holding her fist to her mouth as she thought.

Fifteen minutes later, the four of them entered the building and were escorted into a very spacious room with a large silver carpet right down the middle. On both sides of the room were squads of security guards, not in the way, but close enough if needed.

Against the opposite wall were two thrones, each the same size and situated side-by-side. Sitting on them were two people, one male and one female, both who seemed to be in their thirties, and were holding hands.

The woman, who was sitting in the throne on the right had a small smile, had long blond hair like Emmy's. However, the woman's figure was more mature and curved, except that her chest was somewhat small. Her eyes were a startling silver-gray, though there was something about them that seemed slightly unnatural.

She was wearing a knee-length silver-gray dress, the upper part of which had a zipper with three diamonds sewn into each side. In addition, there was a slight hint of light blue under that dress, in the form of light-blue leather armor. And to top it off, she was wearing a silver tiara on her head. Sitting on the arm of her chair was a beautiful young phoenix, blood red in color, with small traces of yellow.

The man, who was sitting in the throne on the left had a knowing smile on his face, and had the same blond hair as the woman's, though it was much shorter. While he wasn't overly buff or thin, his clothing did suggest a better-than-average physique. Like the woman's, his eyes were a startling silver-gray, and had the same subtle unnatural feeling to them.

He wore a silver overcoat, held together in a "zipped" position by a gray belt, which also had three diamonds sewn into each side. He also wore a full-body set of leather armor underneath, only his were dark green in color. Topping it off, he was wearing a silver crown on his head, which was the same size as the woman's tiara.

After stopping five feet away from the thrones, the guards escorting them bowed slightly and retreated a few steps, but still at the ready.

Striding forward a step, Keith swept his hand up and formally bowed to the two figures. "Your Majestie's, I have to deliver to your attention a report on a most troubling matter," he said, straightening up. After the teens' startled reaction, they hastily bowed as well.

But the king slowly stood, his face carefully impassive. "That can wait as you have some explaining to do, Keith" he said in a commanding voice.

He slowly walked down the small steps in front of the throne, scaring the teens slightly while Keith remained completely calm. As soon he was close, the king stopped in front of Keith. He was roughly the same height as Keith, and his impassive face hinted that something was raging.

Then the king playfully punched Keith on the arm.

He laughed then grinned, the commanding tone evaporating. "Keith, you old dog," he said simply. "Why do you always wait till the reports to come visit your old friend?"

Keith simply laughed, holding out his arms for a hug, the king immediately obliging. They chuckled as the two bear-hugged, thumping each other's backs.

Brianna, Emmy, and Veren all stared, dumbstruck.

After they pulled apart, Keith simply grinned as he did a mock bow. "Purely to mess with you," he answered playfully. "In addition to being busy taking care of my school subjects," he said with playfulness, standing up straight. "Something you don't do."

The king mimed a hurt expression, a hand over his heart. "Oh, that stings, Keith" he said in mock pain, then straightened with a grin of his own. "I do take care of my subjects, I'll have you know, and it keeps me busy."

"Of course, Your Majesty," Keith answered, smiling.

"And you know how I dislike formalities!" the king said with a little mocking bow of his own.

Keith threw his head back slightly and laughed, then grinned. "Then one wonders how you became king, Skye."

Before he could retort though, the queen gave a firm cough—and by the practiced sound of it, she had done so quite often.

Skye stopped himself then smiled at Keith. "Clearly, we have a lot to talk about, but now's not the time," he said, going back to command. "You said you had a report?"

But before Keith could speak, a guard entered from one of the side rooms, saluted. and proceeded to announce: "Your Majestie's, Lord Phillip has come with an important discovery, and he must speak to you with all speed."

Skye glanced between the guard and Keith, then smiled. "You don't mind waiting?" he asked as if he knew the answer.

Keith shook his head, his hands behind him. "Not at all, Your Majesty" he said with all courtesy. Despite this, however, somewhere underneath the surprise, Bri saw something flicker in his expression. It was almost as if something was off, and he was trying to find its source.

Skye grimaced a little, but he stepped up the stairs and sat on his throne again, his face impassive.

"Bring him forward," he commanded to the guard, who saluted again and stepped into the side room.

While that had been going on, Brianna and the others slowly got over their shock. "Keith knows the king? And they're friends?" she whispered softly to her friends, who shrugged in confusion as well.

"Sorry, Bri, but we didn't know," whispered Emmy, looking at her. "Not until now."

"Yeah, not at all," said Veren.

"Don't worry, I'll tell you the story later," Keith discreetly whispered to them, startling them.

As soon as Keith finished his sentence, the side door opened and out came a man, dressed in blue clothes with hints of silver. Judging by his slightly frail appearance and somewhat pale skin, he had the look of someone who spent all his time indoors. Despite that, his brown eyes and expression said that he wasn't to be messed with, and nobody doubted that message from the sword he carried at his belt.

As he stopped in front of the thrones, his brown-black hair moved slightly as he formally bowed.

"Your Majestie's," he spoke, his voice firm and blunt. "I and my scientists have achieved an important breakthrough, one that will change the balance of power of this unofficial war."

Eyebrows were raised, and more than a few mutterings broke out among the guards.

"This is good news" the queen spoke up, looking at Phillip with her hands crossed. "But tell us, what have you actually achieved?" Her voice was soft, yet commanding. The phoenix trilled softly at that moment, and it was the most beautiful sound they had ever heard. It brought a smile to everyone's face, even if only briefly.

Nodding slightly, Phillip continued, "What we have achieved is a new breed of creature, one that will help us in this war. A counterpart, if you will, to the Oblivions that run wild out there." When he finished, he held out his hand, which began glowing a dull purple-black, raising a few murmurs here and there.

Suddenly, an Oblivion appeared, right over where he held his hand.

Brianna screamed in shock and scrambled away from it, stumbling against something warm, instantly gripping its arms tightly.

After a few startled breaths, she slowly realized that the Oblivion wasn't really there. Sure it looked solid, behind this small glowing circle holding it back, and doing every single scary and creepy thing it always did—but it lacked the aggression that would have made it try to escape its holdings. She slowly realized this Oblivion was a fake—no threat and just for show, but that didn't help her nerves.

Acting as if nothing happened, Phillip extended his other hand outward and it began to glow too, only blue white this time. A circle of light appeared on the ground, and the air around it slowly became charged, making Brianna grip even harder. When the charging finished, the light became it's brightest yet. After it cleared away and everyone had looked back, they were all stunned into speechlessness.

The thing standing before them was much like an Oblivion, and yet at the same time, it wasn't.

While its body shape and height were exactly the same as an Oblivion's, and it had the same never-stop-moving trait—but somehow more graceful than jerky—the glowing eye color was a pure, intense blue instead of dark gold. The color of its skin was a near-blinding white, with small veins of silver flowing up and down. It even had two small antennae like those of an Oblivion, except white in color. With a low half-hissing, half-sizzling sound—which was somehow softer than the Oblivion's—thick swirls of white sparkles constantly radiated from it's body.

The most notable feature, though, was the pair of silver wings that the creature sprouted from its back. They were angelic and a little feathery, and twice its body size. The wings moved the same way the creature did—never staying still, even for a second. Small air currents constantly swirled around the wings.

To say that everyone was surprised would have been an understatement, though Phillip's expression didn't change. The king and queen themselves couldn't suppress their excitement, though they did ask the expected questions, and Phillip was happy enough to oblige. In the process, the creatures had been named Oathkeepers, and when asked why they were named so, Phillip had replied that it just seemed appropriate.

During this, Brianna finally figured out whose arms she was gripping— Veren's. Naturally, this little realization had made her blush deeply, and even more so when she thought that he hadn't minded at all!

Neither did she, when she thought about it.

Finally, after the king and queen had asked everything they had wanted to and sent Phillip back to the labs, they turned their attention back to Keith, who grimly started the report of what had happened yesterday.

After he'd finished, both the king and queen were stunned. "B-but that can't have happened!" Skye exclaimed, sounding very worried. "We'd have gotten a report about the attack as soon as it happened!"

"I know," said Keith, who sounded grim, "which is why when Phillip was answering your questions, I secretly extracted a few memories from his brain."

The five of them stared at Keith, completely shocked. "You-you did what!?" said Brianna, finding herself shocked, and proud for some reason.

Keith sighed slightly before continuing. "I know it's frowned upon, but I felt it was necessary," he said, looking up at them. "There was a complete lack of tension in the air here, which should have been thick from the attack, so I got suspicious. And what I found was completely disgusting." Keith shook his head, his expression disgruntled.

"Phillip was outside the castle, witnessed the attack, then decided that his experiments were far more important," he continued grimly. "So he erased all the memories of the attack from the guards, and the memories of the insistent people who tried to tell you, so that nobody would interfere with his work."

Shocked silence filled the room, except for small mutterings from the guards from this little revelation.

"That guy is in some serious trouble for that little stunt," Skye muttered to himself, but loud enough for the others to hear.

The queen leaned forward, her expression tight. "Guards, find and detain Lord Phillip until further notice," she said tensely. "We'll call for him later."

Four of the assembled guards bowed and left. Her phoenix trilled sadly, but it was still a beautiful note.

Skye cleared his throat, sitting up straight. "Anyway, there is another order of business that needs solving," he said carefully. "Due to the atrocities our security forces have committed, they have been removed, which leaves us with vacancies to fill."

"And I'm thinking, until we find suitable replacements, your students will fill those spots."

Keith smiled slowly, while in the background, the three teenagers blinked several times in surprise. "Somehow, I expected this, Your Majestie's," he said, bowing. "I'll be sure to inform them about everything they need to know."

A little later, still in surprise about finding herself as security now, Brianna turned to leave with her friends.

"Bri? Can you please stay a little longer?"

Very surprised now, Brianna stopped, looking at the queen that at her friends. "Um, I guess I'll catch up with you" she said, making a small noise.

Emmy hugged her for a moment, letting go after a bit with a small smile. "See you then," she said simply, already turning to go. And it wasn't hard to miss how the smile vanished the moment she turned away.

Her heart sank as she watched her go. She really didn't like how she saw a glimpse of the old Emmy, but it disappeared almost as soon as she turned around.

Veren sighed as he watched Emmy go, then he looked at Bri. "Don't worry, she'll be back to normal soon," he said, but she almost instinctively knew that he didn't really believe it.

She nodded slowly. "Yeah, I'm sure she will" she said, knowing deep down it wouldn't be that simple.

Veren nodded then raised his fist, holding it up. Bri bumped her fist back, feeling a bit warm as she watched him go for a few moments. Then she turned and headed toward the throne, where the queen was beckoning her.

Skye excused himself from the conversation, saying he needed to get in a bit of training so his skills wouldn't get rusty. This surprised her, but the queen had asked her to stay, not Skye.

"So, Brianna, I hear you've really got a grudge against these former guards, even from when you were six years old" said the queen, gently stroking the phoenix's feathers as it perched on the throne's left arm, to it's softly trilling. A ring glittered on the queen's finger.

Brianna blinked, but before she could ask, the queen beat her to the punch: "Keith has told me *a lot* about you, Bri—more than he has told you yet"

Brianna blinked several times and finally found her voice. "W-What do you mean, Your Majesty? What is he not telling me?"

The queen smiled at her. "Call me Jeena, Bri. It's okay" she said gently, then her smile widened. "As for Keith, he'll tell you when he's good and ready, and it will be a pleasant surprise for you"

Brianna nodded slowly, not sure what to say to that. "Okay-"

"Oh, and Bri?" Jeena said, tilting her head.

"Y-yes?" she asked hesitantly.

Jenna's smile became mischievous, and her eyes twinkled. "Don't keep that boy waiting too long. He's *so* into you, and you are too. I can tell." she said, winking at her.

Brianna blushed and her heart raced at the thought, but all she could do was to be respectful. Making a slightly shaky bow, she said, "Thank you, Your Maj—Jeena," and hurried out, not hearing Jeena's small chuckle of amusement.

A NEW JOB

July 2, 2027

"I can't believe we were given these jobs" Bri said faintly, climbing up the wall's built-in stairs. Emmy and Veren followed behind her. "I'm not sure what to say about it."

"Never had one before, Bri?" Veren asked from behind her.

She breathed out faintly, looking upward. "No, but I never had *anything* normal before I met you and Emmy," she whispered.

"True," Veren admitted, then he looked back at Emmy. "What do you think, Emmy? About us getting these jobs?"

"I think they'll take away from our training," she answered, rather offhandedly. "And our efforts to find the Guards."

Veren tried to steer the conversation back around, but everytime he did, Emmy would sort of tune it out.

To Brianna's surprise, Veren gripped her arm, stopping her from moving up more stairs, while Emmy just walked past them. "We have to do something about this," he whispered quickly in an undertone. "Emmy is a completely different person. And I don't like it one bit!"

She breathed out faintly, glancing up at Emmy. "Yeah, she is," she whispered back, worried. "But what can we do? I don't think anything but Setxis himself would be good enough for her."

"Then, maybe we can curb it a bit," he whispered, letting go of her arm slowly. "You know, take out her aggression and hatred on Oblivions or something."

Brianna slowly smiled a bit; that idea had potential.

Minutes later, they walked up the stairs, and found themselves at the top of the wall.

"Quite a view," Veren breathed, whistling.

"Yeah," Brianna agreed, though she was looking at Emmy, who sat on top of the stonework, watching the ground below only vaguely. She sighed inwardly, rubbing her head.

"Don't worry, we'll get her back to normal," Veren said, standing beside her.

She nodded, looking back at him with a smile. "I know," she said simply.

To her surprised curiosity, Veren started fidgeting a bit, and he actually blushed a little. "Hey, Bri?" he whispered, tilting his head. "I also have this idea that might help you."

"About what?" she asked, blinking.

"About your fear of Oblivions," he said nervously, rubbing his head a little.

"Huh?" she breathed, blinking several times.

October 2, 2027

It was a warm autumn day in Liark, warmer than it should have been. The sun was still high in the sky, casting its bright light over the busy city. But while the city was busy, it was quiet outside the outer wall—almost too quiet for them.

"Oi" Brianna sighed, sitting up against the outer wall. "How much longer till our shift's over?"

She wore her usual training outfit, which was mainly a white shirt and black shorts along with a dark-blue half-jacket, two different symbols on the sides. Completing the outfit was a pair of silver sneakers.

"About an hour" Veren said, lying flat on his back, also sounding bored. As they had discovered, keeping watch for outside threats consisted largely of boredom—something they were not used to.

He was also wearing his training outfit, which consisted mainly of a red shirt and silver shorts. Over his black-zippered red shirt, he was wearing a gold half jacket. Completing the outfit, he had on a pair of light-blue sandals.

"I should be in one of the other groups, looking out for *him*," Emmy muttered, sitting on top of the higher stonework.

Like her friends, she wore her training outfit as well, which consisted mainly of a low-cut fuchsia dress—which was short enough that it didn't hamper her movements—and a pair of blue shorts underneath that. There was a light-green shirt underneath her dress, which went well with her pair of maroon high-tops.

Veren looked up at her, his expression faintly worried. "We'll be part of that group on our shift tomorrow, Emmy," he said, then looked over at Bri. "And Bri, it's not completely bad. We're bored, but at least we're bored together."

Brianna smiled at him, glancing down at her feet. Soon though, she realized what he'd actually said—the way he'd said we're. "U-uh-"

Veren seemed to realize what he'd said too, and he began to stutter slightly, sitting up. "W-what I meant was, well—uh, it's not so bad when all of us are here, together," he said, rubbing his head.

There was a silence between them—until it was broken by a small giggle.

"You two are so sweet, both stuttering," Emmy teased them.

This statement caused both of them to stutter even more, as well as mentally sigh in relief; the old Emmy was still there underneath.

Giggling slightly again, Emmy laid herself down again with a small smile. Almost instantly though, she snapped upright along with her two friends. They all heard the same dreaded sound.

An all-too-familiar half-hissing and half-sizzling sound.

Summoning her warpblade instantly, Brianna stood up in less than a second, while her two friends scrambled to their feet. "They're down there! They're climbing up the wall!" Emmy exclaimed lightly.

"Oh no, we're not gonna—" Veren groaned as he touched his stomach, but he was cut off by Brianna, who was applying her brand of magic to her feet. "We fight them on the wall, and that's that," she said, then she got a running start and jumped off the outer wall.

The sheer exhilaration of free-falling was indescribable, but even as she enjoyed it's feeling, she kept her eyes down below at the wall-scaling Oblivions.

Soon enough, she flipped herself in mid air and faced her feet toward the wall. Coated with magic as they were, they magnetically pulled her against the wall. Sliding down for a few seconds, she stopped after slowing herself down. It also protected her from any harmful effects her shoes would have gotten otherwise.

Standing there on the wall, she stared down at the approaching Oblivions. She felt fear in the back of her mind, but she also felt the adrenaline of battle overpowering it. As per Veren's advice, and repeated sessions with Oathkeepers, she soon looked at them with hatred instead.

Soon enough, she found herself joined by Emmy and Veren. Veren looked uneasy, but that was more from the fact that he looked a little green.

After that, the first few Oblivions reached them, one of them leaping up and slashing a claw at Brianna. She dodged-rolled on the wall, got her feet back on it, then jumped off. She slashed her way through several of them, falling a short distance before her magic reattached her to the wall.

She scanned the area around her: while Emmy and Veren were occupied with their own small groups, she noticed a larger group climbing up from a hundred feet below, approaching rapidly.

With a small smirk, her hand began glowing bright white, and she lightly slammed her palm against the wall. The white magic shot out and formed a sun shape around her, rapidly connecting and filling the gaps with bright light. The sun-shaped symbol shot out glowing white lines, racing down the wall toward the larger group of Oblivions, gracefully curving their way.

The Oblivions hissed as soon as the glowing lines came near them, and even more so when Oathkeepers sprouted up from them.

With heavy hisses, light and darkness clashed against each other, attacking each other viciously. Screeches split the air as the two sides fought. An Oblivion's tendrils would lash out and grab an Oathkeeper, putting its electricity to good use. The Oathkeeper's wings would slam the Oblivion hard against the wall, using the wind for good measure. And all through it, the Oblivions and Oathkeepers were at each other's throats, with teeth and claws alike.

All this and more happened within the span of a few seconds, which Brianna had been watching. Having a number of Oathkeepers under their command helped.

She slashed through an Oblivion that had been trying to sneak up on her, then she turned her attention back to the smaller group.

Emmy and Veren were handling different smaller groups of Oblivions, but she saw another part of the group starting to sink into the wall, obviously going for a surprise attack. *Not on my watch* she thought with a slight scowl.

"Hey, ugly!" she shouted at the group of Oblivions, which stopped them and made them look around in confusion. In her mind, she saw not Oblivions, but Setxis's face.

Holding her warpblade tightly, she raised it high so that they could see. "Yeah, I'm talking to you!" she continued to yell, not noticing the slight glow that was appearing around her. "I'm standing right here! What are you waiting for!?"

This angered them, and with a hiss, they rushed at her. She took up a battle— ready position, the glow getting stronger and stronger by the second. "You want me? Come and get me!"

The glow became it's strongest yet, then faded away. She had gained her defiance drive.

Her training outfit had turned orange with gray accents, and she had glowing blue energy streams circling her. Her original warpblade had changed to an *attack* warpblade, and she had gained a second magic warpblade in her left hand. Whenever she moved her warpblades, the energy streams would circle them instead.

Finally noticing the fading glow, Brianna glanced down at herself. She'd been trying to goad the Oblivions into attacking, but this was unexpected.

Then she slowly grinned at the Oblivions. She didn't say a word, but she held both her warpblades in a reverse grip. She waited a few seconds then let loose on the attacking Oblivions.

At first, other than the second warpblade, she saw no real difference from her normal fighting style. It wasn't important to find out right at that very second, but it still bothered her.

Finally, she was down to her last few Oblivions, and she faced them. Slashing her way through two, she grasped both her warp-blades hard and did a, over-the-head looping attack, which the last Oblivion was too slow to avoid. Her warpblade went right through it, dissolving it instantly while the momentum continued it's path downward.

Boom!

The sheer force of the blow did more than impact the stone wall. It *cracked*, and the cracks spread in a twenty-five-foot radius.

Brianna panted slightly from the blow, not noticing the outcome immediately.

She blinked slowly, just standing there in shock, staring down at what she had done by accident. "Oh my—" she whispered faintly, dazed. Completely unnoticed, both her warpblades and her defiance drive disappeared in flashes of light. She didn't even notice the drain on her mental endurance.

"Uh—Bri? Did you do that?"

Brianna was startled, looking around to find Emmy slowly walking toward her on the outer wall, staring at her cracked-wall handiwork. But she immediately noticed that Veren wasn't here though. "Uh—I think, but, where's Veren?" she asked.

Emmy shook her head with a slightly rueful expression, gesturing her head upward. "As soon as the Oblivions were gone, he turned green and went back to level ground as fast as he could," she said, her attention turning back to the cracked wall.

Brianna looked down slightly and smiled. She started to walk back up to the top of the outer wall, but Emmy's comment stopped her. "Uh, Bri? What about the wall?"

Brianna slowly looked back around, looking at the cracked section of the wall. For several seconds, there was no sound but the wind.

Then Brianna grabbed Emmy's wrist, to both their surprise. "What they don't know won't hurt us," she whispered quickly. Then without hesitation she ran up the outer wall, dragging the surprised Emmy with her.

On the way up, she could have sworn Emmy made a comment about how much the damage would cost.

Up on the outer wall, after they had removed their magnetic magic, they found Veren slightly leaning against the wall, still looking green. Nevertheless, he stood up straight when they came close, smiling faintly. "Hey, girls, what's new?" he said.

"I just got my defiance drive" Brianna said with a smile, to the surprise of her two friends. "Really? I didn't see you turn into a *drive*, Bri," said Emmy, tilting her head slightly.

Brianna smiled as she shook her head a bit. "It faded before you could get a look, Emmy. I'll show you both later, once this shift is over," she said, getting nods from both of them.

With less than an hour left, they once again fell into a lull, but not nearly as bored as usual.

PLANS

October 9, 2027

Brianna sighed, lying there on the outer wall with her eyes closed, completely bored as usual.

Sure, she and her friends had taken care of a group of Oblivions earlier, but other than that, this particular job was long stretches of nothing. She just wasn't cut out to do this, and she was beginning to wonder how long they would need to fill in.

Well, at least we're getting paid she thought, slowly opening her eyes. *And we still get to train every 3rd day.*

A cloudy sky greeted her as she opened her eyes, and she sighed again, looking to her right.

Veren leaned against the wall, looking as bored as she felt, while Emmy took her turn keeping watch. Bri couldn't see her expression from this angle.

Veren saw her looking at him, and inside, she felt a little afraid he'd think she was staring at him. But to her relief, he smiled slightly, giving her a nod that he knew how she felt—bored.

Afterward, he glanced in the other direction for a moment, then he sat up quickly, surprised.

"Hey, girls," he said, getting their attention. "We have a visitor," he said. Both girls looked around. After the surprise, they quickly stood up.

Keith stood there, smiling at them with a curious look. "Hey, you three, how's work going?"

"Boring, most of the time," said Veren, glancing at Brianna and Emmy.

Keith himself chuckled slightly, smiling. "Well, I might know a way to relieve that boredom," he said, turning slightly. "Just follow me to the school, and we'll talk there."

"But we're doing our jobs, we can't just abandon it," Bri said, dusting herself off slightly as she sat up.

Keith's smile fell slightly. "It involves the guards, and-".

"What! Why didn't you say so? Let's go!" Emmy yelled, already running past Keith.

"Come on," said Keith after a moment, turning and walking toward the school. Brianna and Veren followed him, rubbing their heads. They shared a pained look between them.

They were dreading this upcoming talk now because of Emmy's reaction. And they feared it might have reversed part of their plan's results.

"We've finally found the guards. Their hiding place is the same place as before; their underground tunnel system," said Keith during the briefing.

Emmy, whose face was dark and whose arms were crossed, simply scoffed and muttered under her breath, "I could have told you *that*."

Her two friends looked at her with worried faces, then at each other with the same look.

"Well, why haven't you found them before now, Keith?" asked Emmy, her tone cold.

Keith acted as if he hadn't heard her tone. "That's simple. Because the city's other security forces were searching everywhere else," he said, glancing between them. "It wasn't until recently that they asked me to help them, and I thought they might be stupid enough to hide in the same area," he continued, looking at Emmy directly. "But unfortunately, I haven't found their main area in that underground tunnel system yet."

"Then I volunteer to help search, Keith" said Veren, stepping forward, much to Bri's surprise.

Keith nodded, smiled slightly. "I'm sure you can do it, Veren."

"Hey, wait a minute!" Emmy protested heatedly, stepping forward and shoving Veren aside. "I'm the one with a grudge here! Let me instead!"

Keith started to explain, and Emmy started arguing. As this went on, Veren slowly backed away from the argument, lightly massaging where Emmy had shoved him. He quickly found that Brianna had stepped toward him.

"Are you sure you want to do this, Veren?" she whispered in concern, standing close to him.

Veren smiled gently at her, slowly and gently putting an arm around her shoulder. "Don't worry. I'll be fine, Bri," he whispered gently, smiling. "Even if they do catch me, they can't fight that well, so I'll be fine."

"And also—" he whispered in a low tone, glancing at the still-bickering Emmy, "Emmy will need some cheering up, and I thought you would be best for that."

Brianna smiled faintly, touched. "Okay," she whispered gently, but still concerned. "Just be careful, okay?"

Veren smiled, holding her closer with his arm, making her blush more. "I will. Don't worry. Now, wish me luck, Bri," he whispered gently.

"Good luck" she whispered, meaning it as she smiled at him. Meanwhile, her heart was racing just from his arm being around her shoulder.

There was a moment's silence between them. Suddenly, he leaned forward, kissing her on the cheek. She gasped aloud. Veren took his arm off her shoulder at that same moment, quickly making his way over to Keith. He had finally stopped Emmy's arguing, and then he and Veren started talking, obviously discussing the plan. Despite the serious talk, Veren seemed slightly dazed by what he'd done, a little red even.

Brianna just stood there, her mouth slightly open and her face a deep crimson, feeling as though her heart were about to explode. Her right hand unconsciously touched the spot where Veren had kissed her.

Moving beside her, Emmy was muttering to herself, "I try to get revenge and what does he do? He says no *and* makes sure that I can't," she said, huffing in frustration.

Eventually, she looked at Brianna. She slowly tilted her head as her eyebrows furrowed, looking at the deep blush and hand over her cheek. She glanced over at Keith and Veren, the latter having a slight blush still visible, then back at Brianna. "Bri?" she asked.

Brianna gave no reaction.

Emmy waved her hand in front of Bri's face. Still no reaction. *Hmm, interesting,* she thought to herself, then smiled slightly. *Okay . . . time to kick it up a notch"*

She got her lips close to Brianna's ear. "Hey, Bri!" she yelled lightly, thoroughly startling her.

"What the hell, Emmy?" Brianna yelled in irritation, staring at her as she rubbed her assaulted ear.

Emmy placed her hands on her hips "Do you love Veren or not, Bri?" she asked simply.

Brianna blinked rapidly as shock settled in. "What—I-" she sputtered as she tried to get her thoughts together.

All throughout her sputtering, Emmy kept her hands on her hips, she giving Brianna a look.

Finally, Brianna's sputtering faded away. "Y-yes—I do," she whispered softly, blushing deeper. "A-a lot, Emmy"

"I thought so," said Emmy with a small smirk, coming closer and putting her arm around her shoulder.

"W-why did you ask?" Brianna whispered, looking at her.

Emmy continued to smirk for a moment. "Because it's more than obvious that you two love each other," she whispered gently. "And also, it's sorta painful to see you not together yet."

Rubbing her head, Brianna looked down slightly. "Well, it's just—I want to, but there's so much else going on" she whispered, barely audible at times. "It just—it doesn't seem like the right time, even though my heart lights up every time he so much as looks at me"

Emmy briefly looked up in thought, then back at Brianna. "Well, how about you wait just a little bit longer?" she whispered gently, her head tilted. "Till all your distractions are out of the way, then you make your move with Veren. Or until he makes his move, whichever you prefer"

Brianna slowly looked up, but she didn't answer.

To tell the truth, she'd known she was in love with Veren for some time, as well as vice versa. But like she had said, there never seemed to be a right time. And in addition, there was her own nervousness in the way.

A Secret

Brianna couldn't stop pacing.

Beside her, Emmy sat against the school wall, watching her walk back and forth. "Relax, Bri. Veren can take care of himself," she said, but this got no reaction from Brianna.

Sighing, she leaned back against the wall, then smirked slightly after a few moments.

"Hey, Bri, while we wait, I know just the thing to do," she said with the same smirk. "Think of your couple name when you and Veren get together."

Brianna stumbled and gasped, turning around quickly to stare at Emmy.

Oblivious to this, Emmy continued with a smirk. "Now let's see—Brianna and Veren together, what does that make?" she whispered, humming in thought. "I got Brieren and Veranna, but Veranna sounds much better, personally. What do you think, Bri?"

"S-stop it, Emmy!" she whined a bit, her face impossibly red.

But deep down, she couldn't deny it; the second one had sounded much better. And in the back of her mind, she was glad Emmy was acting a bit like her old self.

The sounds of talking soon intruded upon their thoughts, and both girls looked in the direction they came from. In the distance, two people were walking toward them, but one was limping noticeably. As they came closer, they revealed themselves to be Keith and—

"Veren!" she cried out, instantly running toward them, followed shortly by Emmy.

Veren walked with a limp toward them, panting as the girls helped him sit down, though he winced a bit from his bruises. Keith remained a slight distance away while Emmy got herself down on her knees and started working healing magic over Veren's legs, despite her inexperience with it.

Brianna found herself fixing up Veren's hair, looking at him worriedly. "What happened to you, Veren?" she said in concern.

Veren grimaced somewhat from his bruises as he spoke. "I got jumped. I got away, but not without some bruises, sadly," he said, stifling a groan. "They've gotten better, much better than I expected," he said, shaking his head a bit, exposing a rather nasty cut on his left cheek.

She gasped slightly, and without knowing it, Brianna found her left hand cupping Veren's cheek.

As soon as they realized it, both blushed hard. "Uh—Bri? What are you doing?" Veren stammered, his face heating up.

She didn't answer, not trusting herself to speak. To cover herself, she focused, and her hand began glowing green. Veren's cut began to heal.

It did nothing to help ease their mutual embarrassment. Both of them looked down slightly, silent. Bri was secretly enjoying the slight touch of his cheek though, further embarrassing herself.

Thankfully, Emmy broke that with her question. "So Veren, did you find out where they are exactly?"

After blinking slightly at the interruption, he looked over to Emmy and nodded. "Yeah, I did," he said. "Like Keith said, they're hiding out in their underground tunnel system. They must have been using magic of some sort to conceal their location. Otherwise, they couldn't have hid there for so long undetected," he continued, glancing at Bri.

That one glance told her that he was still worried about Emmy's hatred, which she agreed with.

Going to the one place where the hatred had all began was *not* going to be good, and that was an understatement.

"And now that we know exactly where they are—the root of this city's problems—you'll need plans," Keith spoke up, and who stepped closer to the three of them. "But before that, you'll need some training to boost your rusting skills, just in case you need them."

They all agreed to that, but when Keith ran off to attend to a problem with a few students, Veren brought up an important point.

"Wait, we're supposed to be doing our jobs. We can't just ditch it" he said, his eyebrows furrowed.

"Who cares?" Emmy said coldly. "They're all going down"

There was silence among the three of them. For their friendship's sake, Brianna and Veren ignored it.

"Actually, we *are* doing our jobs" Brianna said slowly in realization. "We're protecting the city from threats. Nobody said we had to stay on the outer wall to do it."

Veren stared at her while Emmy merely smirked.

"—That's devious," said Veren, slowly grinning. "I like it," he whispered with glee, making Brianna blush a bit—or a lot.

October 11, 2027

Brianna stood there in her resistance drive, facing off against Emmy and Veren. She held her warp-blades in a reverse-grip, ready for the onslaught they were going to throw at her. Emmy and Veren stood opposite her about fifteen feet away, with Emmy in her defiance drive and Veren in his mind drive.

For a few seconds, only the wind moved. Then, Emmy and Veren moved at the same time, their hands glowing four different colors: red and yellow for Emmy, light green and blue for Veren.

From Emmy's left hand, several large fireballs were shot at her. From her right hand, a lightning bolt struck down from the sky and split apart, coming straight at her. From Veren's left hand, a large whirling sphere of air formed and moved fast toward her. From his right hand, a whirlwind of frost came straight at her.

Brianna merely smiled at the elemental onslaught, holding up her warp-blades in an X pattern. There was a tremendous explosion, the four elements mixing surprisingly well. When the smoke cleared, Brianna merely stood there, without a scratch.

"Not bad, you two. I actually felt a little of that," she said, smiling a bit as she dusted herself off.

With three flashes of light, the three friends changed out of their drives with the expected slight staggering from mental drain. Veren went to get a bite to eat, and Brianna went with him; while Emmy stayed, practicing some of the movements and forms.

Inside the school, Brianna grabbed an apple and took a bite out of it, making a surprised sound when Veren took her aside. "There's something you should know about what I found out," he whispered discreetly, making her look at him curiously.

"Like what?" she whispered back, glancing around.

After glancing around himself, he looked back at her. "Well, when I was there, I spied upon a meeting with Setxis and a lot of other guards. While I was doing so, I noticed that every single one of them had all-black eyes," he whispered quieter.

She knew instantly what that meant—they were all possessed.

But Veren wasn't done. "But, I noticed something else. Setxis did *not* have all-black eyes, not at any point."

Brianna blinked several times in shock, her mind immediately reeling about the implications. "That means—" she whispered slowly in shock, "someone else is behind the guard's atrocities. Except for Setxis."

She looked down, barely believing what she'd heard.

Veren looked down as well, whispering, "Yeah."

After a while, something else occurred to Brianna, and she looked up at Veren. "Wait, why aren't you telling Emmy this?" she whispered slowly, tilting her head.

Veren glanced around, and this time he stepped closer, making her blush slightly. "Because," he whispered firmly but quietly. "You and I both know Emmy won't listen right now. Her heart is filled to the brim with pure hatred against them, and she needs to let it out, or she'll never be the same again."

Brianna slowly nodded reluctantly, but she remained worried. "But, what if she—" she whispered weakly, stopping herself. She didn't want to say it.

"We'll make sure she gets Setxis, no one else," he whispered quietly in determination, making her look at him. "After all, he's the one who started this whole thing, nearly a—assaulting Emmy. The others may have been part of it, but it wasn't entirely their fault."

Brianna slowly nodded, sighing weakly, then she looked at Veren. "So, when will we go after the Guards?" she whispered quietly.

Veren sighed slowly, looking at her with what seemed to be dread. "The day after we've built up our skills," he whispered, looking down. "Five days—five days, and Emmy will go berserk upon Setxis."

Neither one of them said anything, but they shuddered simultaneously.

The release of Emmy's hatred all at once—it was not something they wanted to see in this lifetime, let alone at all.

"Yeah" Brianna whispered, looking down. "Setxis is so screwed"

STORMING THE GUARDS

October 16, 2027

"All right guys, we're here," Veren whispered, stopping at the bare small area. Brianna and Emmy stood by him, Emmy glancing around it carefully.

With expressions of faint dread, Brianna's and Veren's hands begin to glow dark blue, encompassing the hidden square. They struggled a bit, but they managed to lift it. After carefully setting it down, Veren slowly stepped down the stairs that led to the tunnel, which had a hint of red light at the bottom.

Brianna was about to follow right behind him, but she was lightly pushed aside by Emmy, who didn't say anything as she went down the stairs.

She put a hand to her forehead, forcing herself to breathe slowly and think. *She's just angry, she'll be fine later,* she thought weakly. *I hope—*

Taking in a breath and letting it out, she followed them down the stairs.

The three friends carefully walked through the tunnel in silence, listening for the slightest sound. Every so often, there was a mounted red lantern that lit the way.

"Okay, we're coming up to the first room," whispered Veren, which the two girls nodded at. Going a bit more slowly, Veren checked if the coast was clear, then all three of them stepped into the room. It was just as Brianna remembered it: an underground room with a badly done underground-cave makeover.

Veren slowly sighed for a moment, which reflected the dread that he and Brianna were both feeling. "This way," he whispered, turning right at the intersection, leading the way.

The tunnels twisted and turned fairly, and they would have gotten lost easily. At least Veren had his map with him, made of actual magic, in case they got lost. He stopped every now and then, checking the map.

They turned a corner and passed a room.

Brianna blinked slowly then glanced backward. Emmy had stopped completely.

"Veren!" Brianna whispered intently, though she was surprised herself.

Several seconds passed as they both stared at Emmy, who was looking into the room, her face intense. Slowly coming closer, Brianna waved a hand in front of her face. Nothing changed, so she slowly looked into the room itself, hoping to understand why.

The realization slammed into her gut with full force.

Her eyes widened, and she turned quickly. "Veren!" she whispered intently. "It's *the* room!" she told him, but his eyebrows furrowed in confusion, so she said, "*The* room! Where *it* nearly happened!".

Veren's eyes widened in horror. "Well, we have to stop her—" he started to yell, only to stop. "She's already entered," he whispered weakly, his face gone slack.

Brianna's heart sank. She slowly turned to look at the door, breathing heavily with fear.

A dark-blue barrier appeared over the doorway, and hints of it could be seen in the room itself, covering the walls. She slowly looked at Veren; his hand was glowing dark blue.

"We-we can't stop her," Veren rasped weakly, sounding helpless. "So—we make sure no one hears anything" he finished, sounding like he wished he were anywhere else.

She agreed wholeheartedly.

Breathing slowly, neither of them daring to move, they just watched the doorway with dread.

The seconds passed agonizingly slow, then suddenly the room flashed with light. The area shook, making them flinch. Brianna unconsciously grabbed Veren's arm in the process. More flashes and shaking followed, then the room practically exploded.

They backed up in alarm when thick black smoke poured out of the room, making them cough heavily.

More seconds passed, what seemed to be an eternity with their dread. Then Emmy stepped out of the room, brushing the small debris off herself.

She looked at them slowly, her eyes blank and emotionless. "That's done," she said. "Let's move on."

The blankness of her tone, as if it were normal, scared them. As they felt this, Emmy slowly raised an eyebrow at them, but didn't say anything.

Brianna and Veren slowly looked down, becoming aware that she was wrapped around his arm. They both slowly pulled away awkwardly. Neither actually minded all that much, but now wasn't the best time.

"Uh, um—sh-shall we continue?" Veren stammered after a few seconds. Bri quickly nodded, rubbing her own arms as Veren quickly led the way, Emmy following before her.

Not soon after, the trio continued onward through the tunnels. They did so in silence, going through more twists and turns than they knew what to do with.

Suddenly, Veren held his arm out, stopping them just as they came near a big room. He held up his other finger for silence, then he crept closer to the wall, listening carefully.

"Okay, the room's empty" he whispered slowly, looking back at them. "This is their main meeting area. They come in every week, and they'll be here soon. We should sneak in and hide ourselves, so we'll be able to listen in."

Brianna glanced around slightly, then looked back at Veren. "Okay, but how?" she whispered.

Veren smiled slightly for a moment, glancing back at the room. "Simple. We'll use a specially-crafted magic," he whispered quietly. "It'll make us blend us into any wall, effectively making us invisible," he continued.

Then he walked inside, leaving Bri to blink once, before she and Emmy followed him after a moment. There wasn't much difference between their meeting room, and the other one that Emmy had destroyed, back when it was still undamaged.

Veren started to say something, but Emmy held up a hand, standing in front of him. "Okay, *where* did you get this magic, Veren?"

Veren looked a little sheepish as he rubbed his head, smiling faintly. "Well, Keith's intelligence network has been perfecting this spell for years, and Keith gave it to me. He thought it might be useful," he whispered softly.

Somewhere in the back of Brianna's mind, she found herself liking Veren even more just for that sheepish look he had. She looked away slightly, shaking her head a little. *Save that for later. This is serious,* she thought to herself.

Veren breathed in and out, now looking serious. "But there is one problem," he whispered quietly, sighing. "If I run out of magic, it will wear off and we'll be caught."

"Any way we can prevent that?" Emmy cut in before Brianna got a chance to open her mouth. She sighed, glancing at Emmy and wishing this were over already.

Veren glanced down slowly. "Well, if we held hands together," he whispered faintly, like it might be a bad idea. "It would last longer and better than with just me."

Brianna blushed at the idea of her and Veren holding hands, but Emmy cut in again: "Veren, you know I'm all for this, but I am *not* having you drain all my magic. I'm gonna need it for later, and you know it."

Veren nodded slowly, sighing a bit. "Well—you can be on the end of the link holding Bri's hand, only losing your energy if mine and Bri's are gone," he whispered, gesturing a bit.

Brianna glanced down slightly, the thought still on her mind. Out of the corner of her eye, she saw Emmy glance at her. Her expression didn't change at all, but it still gave her the impression of a knowing glance.

Veren continued after a moment. "Since this magic will take most, if not all of our magic, we should only use it when we're seconds away from being discovered," he whispered intently.

Suddenly, they heard faint footsteps—and many of them, by the sound of it.

"Quick, up against the wall!" he whispered urgently, and they hurried to do so. "Now hold hands," he whispered again, quickly grabbing Bri's hand, while Bri faltered for a moment because of this, but Emmy got her hand around Bri's even quicker.

Literally seconds before they walked in, Veren's hand began glowing white. The whiteness quickly seeped across his body, and across Brianna and Emmy's as well, due to their linked hands. It temporally blinded them, but once they started blinking, a man walked into the meeting room.

It was the bigger man they had seen a few times before, who they assumed to be the leader.

The commander stopped a few feet into the room, looking around slightly with furrowed eyebrows. It then occurred to Brianna that Veren's magic, while active, was giving off a slight noise.

Please, ignore it, she pleaded silently. *Move on.*

Several seconds went by. Brianna forced herself to breathe slowly. She could have sworn she saw the commander's eyes flick toward where they were.

The commander looked away, walking farther into the room. As soon as he did, more men started walking into the room as well, all wearing the armor that was common among the guards.

Brianna exhaled silently in relief, surveying the common guards. All were men of differing races and complexions, but each one had all-black eyes. *Well—at least they don't discriminate too much,* she thought a little grimly.

At the same time, Brianna felt Emmy's hand clench quite a bit. "Easy," she whispered discreetly to Emmy.

Her hand finally unclenched somewhat. But only somewhat, making her slump. When was this gonna end?

When she turned her eyes back to the guards, she found the commander standing on a slightly raised platform, and the other common guards stood in organized ranks.

"Well, men, these last four months of destruction and mayhem have been fun," he said with no change in expression or tone, his voice a bit deep. "But starting today and tomorrow, we will be turning ourselves in."

To say that Brianna was in shock was the understatement of reality. Even without looking, she knew Veren felt more or less the same way.

Emmy was a different story altogether—she simply looked as if she couldn't process what just happened.

"The order to turn yourselves in will be the last order I'll give you men. For now, take a rest and leave this room. And don't tell Setxis any of this," the commander ordered, getting a toneless agreement from all the assembled guards. Almost as one, they turned and walked out of the room, right by the three of them.

Seconds passed, during which time the commander stood there in silence. Brianna then felt a slight jolt, which she identified as her magic being drained. At the same time, Veren's breathing became a bit heavier.

Then the commander raised his hand, holding it out in front of him, then it glowed purple black. Just as suddenly as the purple-black magic, the commander's eyes suddenly turned all-black as well. He began speaking into his glowing hand, his voice as toneless as ever. "Master, the orders have been given. Today and tomorrow, the guards will be disbanded as you have wished," he said, making all three teenagers blink.

"Excellent," came the unexpected female voice, which made Brianna gasp aloud—or at least, she would have if a hand hadn't gently placed itself over her mouth. After giving a little surprised noise, she made the smallest sound as she realized that it was Veren's hand. Just like his hand she was holding, his hand over her mouth was warm.

But when the mysterious voice talked again, those thoughts were unwillingly pushed to the back of her mind.

"The guards are no longer of any use to me, but one in particular still remains—how do you think we should dispose of Setxis?" she said, her tone thoughtful, though it did pause on Setxis's name.

The commander paused for a few seconds, then continued tonelessly, "Master, perhaps Setxis can be taken down. I am not alone here."

All three teenagers gave a reaction of shock, though Emmy's was subdued.

The mysterious voice hummed slightly, "Very well. Tell him to come here, alone. They will deal with him however they like. Should be quite a show," she said. Then, seemingly to herself, she said, "Perhaps his anti-aging magic will be knocked out too."

The commander ended the communication, then he formed another purple-black ball in his other hand. He spoke in a commanding voice, "Setxis, come to the meeting room immediately. Alone."

With that, he cut off the communication and started walking forward, exiting the room.

Veren groaned after a few seconds, then he fell forward on his knees, both hands clutching his forehead.

"Veren!" Brianna cried out, instantly releasing Emmy's hand and kneeling down next to him. "Are you okay?" she whispered a little weakly, gripping his hand in hers.

Breathing heavily, Veren slowly nodded. "I-i'm fine" he whispered shakily. "I-it's just that—the magic kept worsening my headache, e-even with your magic being drained." He slowly looked down, closing his eyes. "I-I thought I was gonna pass out from it, or worse" he rasped quietly.

She vigorously shook her head, pulling Veren against her shoulder. "What matters is that you're fine now, and you'll recover soon," she whispered gently, nervous at what she was doing.

Veren was nervous as well at being propped up against her shoulder, but he slowly looked at her with a smile.

Emmy knelt down on the floor near them, watching with a small smile. She was happy for them, truly, but she was still really focused on revenge against those damned guards—that and not wanting to be a third-wheel.

Well, I'll make sure that I'm not a third wheel as much as possible, she thought, tilting her head at the two lovebirds. As expected, the two were completely oblivious to her at the moment. Her head snapped up instantly at the sound of footsteps.

She stood up quickly, only for her expression to twist into a snarl.

Setxis had just walked into the meeting room.

BRUTAL FIGHT

Setxis walked into the meeting room, looking and sounding disgruntled. "All right, Commander, what did you want?" he said, not noticing the three stunned teenagers to the side.

"You call me over here, and you don't even answer when I ask why. What gives?" he said, trailing off as his gaze fell upon the three teenagers.

Almost instantly, his coal-black eyes narrowed in hatred and disdain. He was already speaking as Emmy stared at him. "What the hell are you three doing here!? You can't possibly have—"

"Shut up," growled Emmy, her eyes literally burning and her snarl frightening. Setxis made the expected retort, but she didn't let him finish as she stepped forward and punched him full in the face, hard.

Setxis landed on the floor roughly, groaning once as he held his face, growling as he struggled to get up.

Emmy merely kicked him back down, staring down at him coldly.

Still in the corner, Brianna and Veren winced.

"Well, he had that one coming" murmured Veren, panting slightly as his shoulders sagged. Her own shoulders did too. The dreaded moment had finally arrived.

"And then some," she murmured back, unconsciously inching backward away from Emmy. "Veren, what will we do?" she whispered helplessly at him, and he slowly looked at her.

"We stay against this wall, and do nothing," he whispered quietly, his eyes filled with quiet dread. "He's had this coming a long time—there's nothing we can do about it"

"And if she goes too far?" she whispered weakly, looking at him with fear. Somewhere in the back of her mind, she was aware of how close they were, but the situation couldn't have been further from that if she tried.

Veren slowly closed his eyes. "If it comes to that—we stop her, Bri" he finally rasped. "There's no other option."

Around the same time, Setxis began standing up, holding his face as he muttered curses. He slowly pulled his hands away, revealing a bruised face and a broken nose, along with burning eyes and a fierce snarl. Both of them paled in comparison to Emmy's.

"You filthy brat!" he yelled in pure rage, drawing his sword and charging at her with an incoherent cry. In a single bound, he was already swinging the sword directly at her head. She didn't so much as blink.

Smack!

Emmy sneered, her burning eyes undiminished as she looked at the now-helpless Setxis. The sword was now caught in her palm in mid-strike. Setxis visibly struggled to do *something*, but to no avail. Emmy, however, was not struggling in the least. Smirking more, she moved her foot back a bit, then threw a well-aimed kick into his crotch.

Setxis pretty much flew across the room, hitting the wall. At the same time, his screech of pain reverberated throughout the room, making Bri and Veren flinch hard.

He curled tightly into a ball on the floor, trembling from the pain, still muttering curses under his breath. Emmy slowly brought up Setxis's sword, holding it horizontally with both hands.

She began to bend the sword, curving it more and more, smirking the whole while. Cracks began to appear while her muscles showed signs of strain.

Setxis's sword snapped with a crystalline sound, small and large shards flying outward. Many of the smaller ones shattered into dust upon impact with the floor, but a few bounced around.

Emmy scoffed slightly. "I expected so much more," she said coldly, throwing the two useless ends away. Setxis slowly stood up, looking at her with hatred written in his face, a little blood trickling from his broken nose now.

Emmy sneered again, staring at him with burning eyes. "You're just another pathetic guard," she whispered icily. "You're nothing and a complete waste of my time."

Setxis's face twisted completely, his control snapped in two. *"Shut up!"* he yelled at full volume, running full speed at Emmy, a fist raised high.

Emmy didn't flinch in the slightest, easily catching his fist with a tight grip. This momentarily stopped Setxis, but with an incoherent cry, he brought his other fist up to strike her. She easily caught that one too, not struggling at all.

Setxis tried to struggle out of the death grip, but Emmy wouldn't budge.

She stared at him darkly, watching him struggle. Her death grip tightened on his wrists, and he cried out as his bones creaked against the unnatural twisting. He struggled harder, but to no avail as Emmy smirked slightly. Her death grip tightened even further, louder creaks intermixing with Setxis's anguished cries.

Crack!

Setxis's scream became a howl, and Emmy finally let go. He staggered back, his wrists soaked with blood, his fingers only twitching. He winced repeatedly as he cradled his broken wrists, the hatred and disdain completely gone from his eyes. In their place, there was only horror and shock.

Emmy's face turned darker. She stepped forward and immediately grabbed his face—using only her hand. By this time, Setxis couldn't put up any kind of a struggle now. Her eyes burning and her snarl frightening, Emmy slowly lifted Setxis up by his face.

The hand holding Setxis began glowing yellow, and Emmy's snarl becoming even more frightening, if possible. Crackling filled the air, then electricity shot out of her hand. Setxis's entire body jerked and twitched, electricity dancing across his body. Dark spots formed around his face, faint whirls of smoke curling off them.

Fifteen seconds earlier

Brianna winced at the slight creaking from Setxis's wrists. "Okay, I think this is starting to go too far," she whispered quickly.

Veren was about to reply, when a hideous crack sounded throughout the room, making them flinch hard.

"Okay, *now* it's gone too far" he said, quickly standing up.

They quickly rushed towards Emmy, but they weren't fast enough to prevent Emmy from electrocuting Setxis.

Both of them tackled Emmy hard, sending her to the ground. Emmy cried out in rage, desperately fighting back, her actions berserk. Brianna held her arms tightly, but it was like trying to keep hold of a twisting snake, with frenzied strength.

"Emmy, stop it!" yelled Veren, managing to hold her from behind, but only for two seconds. "We're your friends!"

One of Emmy's wild swings hit Brianna in the mouth, and she almost blacked out from the pain. Gritting her teeth hard, she ignored the bruise that would be forming shortly and held on to Emmy's arms tightly. "Emmy, don't do this!" she yelled, narrowing ducking under another wild swing. "You're killing him!"

The moment she said *kill*, something seemed to strike Emmy in the gut. She stopped fighting completely, her eyes wide and her breathing coming in heavy pants. She stayed that way for a good while, her friends eventually releasing their grips on her. They sat there quietly, looking at her with deep concern.

What neither of them saw were Emmy's eyes briefly getting an all-black tint, which appeared and disappeared so quickly, they would have dismissed it as their imagination even if they did see it.

Almost immediately, Emmy started tearing up, and she sank down to her knees, burying her face in her hands.

Brianna immediately let go of her arm, cradling the sobbing and broken Emmy, holding her tightly. Veren held Emmy from behind too, his hands on Brianna's back.

For an eternity, they remained in that position. Emmy's sobbing eventually becoming hiccups. Veren very slightly withdrew, standing up and walking a bit beyond them.

Brianna didn't need to ask; she knew he was checking up on Setxis. "It's okay, Emmy. It's okay," she whispered in a raspy gentle tone, cradling her head against her wet shoulder. She kept repeating that line, until Emmy's hiccups faded away, leaving only her whimpers.

"Come on—let's go back" she whispered gently, slowly starting to stand up. Emmy did nothing to help or oppose her; she was just limp, her face still buried against Brianna's shoulder. Bri helped her up the best she could with an arm around Emmy's shoulders, to make sure she would be okay.

Once they were standing, she slowly looked over at Veren. "How is he?" she whispered, not sure what to expect or even what she should feel about Setxis anymore. Even he probably hadn't deserved what Emmy had just dished out.

Veren sighed slightly, looking up at her from his kneeling position. "I'm not sure," he whispered faintly, "but it doesn't look fatal. It might become that though, if he doesn't get expert help."

A pause stretched between them. "Should we take him back with us?" she whispered quietly, thinking of all the terrible things he had done.

Veren slowly closed his eyes, then opened them again as he sighed. "Well—we can't just leave him like this" he whispered finally, his tone showing he understood why she asked that. Then he bent over, carefully hauling Setxis up by the waist, and gently slinging him over his shoulder with a little struggle.

After sighing a bit, Brianna slowly nodded, then they started walking out of the meeting room. They were quiet the whole way, except for Emmy's whimpers.

AMNESIA

It was just after midday at Keith's school, and the weather was nice. Many of the students were outside and enjoying it, but a few were training in it. Three teenagers weren't outside though.

It was relatively quiet inside the medical wing. The only noise was the hustle of the doctors and the occasional sounds of the patients. Brianna stood inside the hospital wing with Emmy, Veren and Keith standing beside her. Together, they looked down at one patient in particular, who was receiving the most attention.

Setxis stirred slightly as the doctors slowly applied healing magic to the burns on his face and his broken wrists, which were currently wrapped up to minimize further damage. Minutes passed as they worked their magic, then Noah stepped away, walking towards Keith.

"How is he?" Keith asked quickly, concerned and serious.

Noah sighed slightly, glancing back toward Setxis. "It's difficult to say exactly," he said, reluctantly. "He'll live for sure, but with the sheer damage he endured, his face may not look the same. His wrists will be fine, once they're healed," he continued, then he hesitated.

"What is it, Noah?" Keith asked grimly.

"He's suffered some damage to his brain, mainly his memory areas," he said at last. "At the very least, he has lost the last ten years of his life."

A deeper silence settled over Keith, Brianna, Emmy and Veren. They had not been expecting that at all.

Noah slowly tilted his head, confusion written over his face. "By the way—what exactly happened to him?"

Keith discreetly glanced behind him, his face neutral. Brianna simply fidgeted in place, her hands together in front of her. Veren fidgeted as well, rubbing his head slowly. Emmy didn't look up, her hair hiding her face.

Keith looked back at Noah, sighing once himself. "I don't know myself, exactly," he said carefully. "And I think that neither of us want to know the details. Trust me."

Noah glanced at the three teenagers himself, then he nodded a little grimly, "Yeah—I guess that would be best."

Suddenly, faint groans were heard from Setxis's bed, with general surprise and shock from the doctors. Everyone's attention snapped around to him instantly.

He slowly looked around, blinking slowly and repeatedly. It was as if he had trouble understanding what he was seeing.

Keith stepped forward and whispered to him in a gentle tone, "Hello there, I'm Keith."

Setxis slowly turned his head toward him, his eyes half-open and blinking slowly. He didn't respond to Keith's greeting.

Still smiling, Keith tried again. "Tell me, do you know these three?" he whispered gently, pointing toward the now surprised teenagers.

Setxis slowly turned his head toward Brianna, Emmy and Veren. Seconds passed with no reaction from him, then he slowly shook his head. "No—" he whispered, his voice weak and hoarse, and with absolutely no trace of disdain. "Not that I remember"

This jolted them all, and those who knew enough about the situation glanced at Emmy. She looked at him with a tortured expression.

After a few seconds of processing this new info, he continued gently, "Well then, do you know anything about yourself?"

Setxis slowly closed his eyes, seconds passing as the effort to remember showed on his face. "N-not much—just a few memories here and there," he whispered hoarsely, with effort. "Of when I was a child—and a name," he continued weakly.

Keith tilted his head, "And whose name is that?" he whispered gently.

"M-mine" he whispered with a struggle. "My name, it's—it's James"

No one said anything, though Brianna, Emmy and Veren continued to stare at Setxis-James in shock.

Eventually, they all left the medical wing as James needed his rest.

"Guys, you go on ahead," Bri said, much to Veren's surprise. Emmy didn't respond or even appear to hear her.

"Why, Bri?" asked Veren, blinking.

"There's something I gotta discuss with Keith," she said, slowly placing her hand on his shoulder. "Please, try to help Emmy, okay?"

He smiled a bit, nodding as he placed his hand over hers briefly. "I will, don't worry," he said gently.

She nodded, but the feel of his hand reminded her of his love lessons.

He left with Emmy while Bri slowly turned around, finding Keith waiting for her expectantly.

"Keith," she said, looking at him. "There's something you should know."

And so she told him about the "anti-aging" comment she had heard, as well as the mysterious female voice.

Keith held a hand to his chin in thought, his expression thoughtful. "I figured someone was behind their actions, considering the black eyes," he said. "Now we know there is someone behind it, along with the gender. Do you remember what her voice sounded like?"

Brianna racked her brains, but for some reason, she couldn't. She remembered the words easily, but the voice kept changing focus. She sighed, rubbing her head. "No, I'm sorry, Keith."

He smiled faintly, nodding. "Well, it's not really important anyway," he decided, then tilted his head. "Besides, now we can focus our remaining security forces to search for this woman."

She nodded, but she found herself thinking about Emmy. What would happen now that she'd gotten her revenge? Would she go back to normal, or would she be changed by what had happened? She fervently hoped for the former.

"By the way," Keith said, jolting her slightly, "you did really well, not just on the mission, but with dealing with Emmy."

She blinked faintly, then giggled weakly. "Thanks," she said. "I was really worried the entire time."

Keith smiled, his tone gentle. "It must have been hard for you."

"You have no idea," she said before she realized it. Without meaning to, she spilled out all her concerns and fears about the whole situation. By the end of it, she was in tears.

"Emmy," she rasped. "I'm afraid. What if she doesn't return to normal?" She's my best friend!"

Suddenly, she was pulled into a hug by Keith. Breathing weakly, she leaned against him, sobbing quietly as she stood there. With her hands wrapped around him, her hands were on his back, while his were on her back and hair. He held her with a gentleness she'd never known before.

"It's okay," he whispered gently, holding her close. "Emmy will be fine, but she needs time. And she needs her friends."

Brianna recovered slowly, her breathing returning to normal. She pulled away slowly, her fingers weakly wiping away her tears.

"I'm—" she whispered weakly, then took a deep breath. "I'm alright."

Keith's smile was tender, almost proud. "I'm glad to here that," he whispered softly. "Now, your friends are waiting for you."

She nodded after a moment, quickly running off. She quickly wiped away her last tears as she did so, not wanting to worry Veren.

She found Veren and Emmy easily as they were simply sitting on the steps of the school.

Emmy, though, had her head on her knees, and Veren was trying to help her.

Brianna slowly approached, sharing a pained look with Veren. She sat down beside Emmy in silence.

"You guys must hate me now," Emmy rasped after awhile.

"Why on earth would we hate you?" Veren asked simply.

"Because of the way I've acted—I was a completely different person. A real jerk even."

"It hurt us to see you like that," Bri admitted, glancing down. "And we were worried sick."

Emmy made a sad sound, burying herself further into her knees.

Brianna looked back at her then put an arm around her shoulder. "But we're your friends," she said weakly. "We stay together, no matter what."

Emmy began to shake and muffled sobs came from her. Bri couldn't tell if they were of relief or sadness, and she glanced at Veren. Veren seemed to understand though; he was smiling weakly, looking between them. In another situation, she would have blushed, but she just felt relieved.

And in that relief, Brianna pulled Emmy and Veren closer, putting them in a three-way hug.

October 17, 2027

It was late in the day, but the sun still shone brightly in the sky.

Brianna lay on top of the outer wall's stonework, staring up into the sky. Veren was leaning against the wall; it was his turn at keeping watch. Emmy sat against the wall near her, knees hugged against her chest, quiet and teary-eyed.

Brianna sighed, her mind still heavy from what they had learned today:

We don't know if he'll make a full recovery on his memory, but he'll look okay in a month or so, they had learned from Noah.

Strangely, the man you knew as Setxis is just gone. It was like that personality was implanted into him, I think. And now it's completely gone, leaving this entirely new person before us, they had learned from Keith, which was the real shocker.

It was difficult for her to imagine, a life without the threat of Setxis looming out there. She had literally grown up with his threat since she was six years old. And now that he was gone, all that was left was the look-alike named James.

I wonder what happened to Set—James? she thought, forcing herself to use his new name. *What happened to make him like the monster that I knew?*

"Vacation time—yeah right" grumbled Veren, jolting her out of her thoughts. She tilted her head upward, looking at Veren, who looked upside down from her angle. Seeing her glance at him, he smiled slightly and looked at her.

"What do you mean, Veren?" she asked, tilting her head in confusion, her knees in the air.

Veren sighed. "Well, while Skye and Jeena approved of our taking down a threat to the city, there was the disregard to our jobs we had done," he said faintly. He rubbed his head slightly. "But, they managed to wave it off as 'vacation time,'" he said, sighing again as he leaned against the wall. "So—we won't be getting a vacation anytime soon, which is a shame."

Brianna made a noise of agreement, wishing they could have some time off as well.

At that moment, Veren blinked, and his eyes brightened. "Wait!" he exclaimed, surprising her as she looked down at him. "Okay, how about this. When we get our next vacation, we can go and visit this special secret spot of mine?" he said, looking at her with a smile.

She slowly smiled back, "Sure!" she said, then tilted her head. "But what is this secret place?"

Veren chuckled, rubbing his head. "That's a secret, of course," he whispered a little deviously.

Unconsciously, she pouted—something she had learned from Emmy (who once taught her what it meant). She tried a few times to get it out of him, but Veren's lips were sealed.

She sighed faintly, figuring she wasn't going to get it out of him anytime soon. "Okay, but what about Emmy?" she asked, slowly sitting up and facing him. "She's feeling guilty right now, and she may not wanna come."

Veren's smile faded, and he glanced at Emmy. "Don't worry," he whispered, but sounded uncertain. "Thanks to what we've done, our next vacation time isn't for six months, and I'm sure that Emmy will work off her guilt by then."

He glanced down, rubbing his head. Brianna slowly got off the stonework, stretching her cramped muscles with a faint groan. "I'm gonna go check on Emmy," she said, walking past Veren, who nodded faintly to show he had heard.

"Emmy?" Brianna whispered faintly, looking down at her. When she got no answer, she slowly sat down beside her, waiting.

"Bri," Emmy rasped eventually, sounding weak.

"Yeah, it's me," she whispered softly, trying not to show the weak part of her voice.

It must have shown anyway, because Emmy made a little sound. "I thought—I thought you and Veren might have second thoughts," she whimpered.

She almost answered, but then realized she didn't know exactly what Emmy meant.

Emmy apparently took her quickly-thinking-about-it silence as something else. "I wouldn't blame you," she continued to whimper, drawing her legs in closer. "But I'd have nothing left."

Those words hit Bri hard, leaving her to stare at Emmy, her own vision blurring for a bit.

Emmy started to shake. "I'm afraid," she breathed, barely audible. "I don't want to be alone—"

Bri herself was crying now, and she swept Emmy into a hug, though a bit awkwardly because of the instinct. Emmy didn't notice—she just began sobbing against her.

January 4, 2028

Bri shivered, quickly breathing twice against her hands, looking around her. She, Veren, and Emmy were at their posts and dressed warmly to ward off the cold. Veren sat against the wall to her left, twiddling with the snow, while Emmy lay on her side about ten feet to the right. So far it had been quiet, but if anything did happen, they'd be able to see it easier because of the contrast against the snow.

Bri was still worried, looking off at her friend. She couldn't tell if their attempts were cheering Emmy up or not, other than the fact that she'd stopped crying.

After a few moments, she realized she heard the crunching of snow close by. She quickly looked around, then up, and got a little nervous.

Underneath his hood, Veren's expression was hesitant, but he was smiling. "Can I sit?"

She didn't follow for a second, then she realized with a jolt that he meant right next to her. "Oh, no, of course," she said quickly, before she realized it. She quickly glanced away nervously, even as Veren slowly did so.

They remained that way for a few minutes, during which Bri's nervousness slowly diminished under her worry. "Hey, can I ask you something?"

He looked at her. "What about?"

She had to struggle against the sudden bout of nervousness. "Well, uh," she stammered, then forced that away. "About Emmy, why is she so—" she continued, only to trail off.

What was the word?

Veren merely raised an eyebrow, turning toward her slightly.

"Clingy?" she finally asked, feeling bad, but knowing no other word that could describe it.

Far from being surprised or shocked, Veren slowly glanced at Emmy, his hood briefly obscuring her view of his face. Then he sighed. "Remember what Emmy mentioned about her family?" he asked, his tone heavy.

She glanced down for a moment. "That they're alive, uh, but never around," she breathed slowly. "And her feelings about them are mixed?"

He nodded. "More-or-less," he answered faintly, glancing at Emmy again. "As merchants, they have to travel a lot, and therefore can only visit rarely. So therefore, her friends—us and Keith—they're all she's got really."

While this twisted her heart, it also made something click in her head. "And she fears being alone," she breathed weakly, looking down. "Emmy told me," she added, seeing Veren's slightly confused expression.

He sighed heavily. "It does fit," he said, looking at Emmy, who slowly glanced over at them. But after a moment, her face was hidden again.

Bri placed her hands together. "Do you think she'll be happy again?" she asked, slightly weak from worry.

Veren looked back at her, then placed a hand on her shoulder, to her slight jolt. "She will," he said gently, but with some strain. "It'll just take some time."

"It's already taken some time!" she cried, surprising both of them.

"I'm sorry," she breathed quickly, looking down. "I just want Emmy back."

A moment's silence, then Veren drew her into a hug, stunning her a little. "So do I," he breathed softly.

Feeling herself blush, she slowly returned the hug, but a bit awkwardly because of the coats. What neither saw was that Emmy looked over at them the moment he hugged her.

There was the faintest hint of a smile, for a moment.

SECRET SPOT

April 19, 2028

The sun was high in the sky, the three teenagers walking down the wall's built-in stairs.

"It's a good thing our shift ended early," Veren said, walking briskly. "Now we can go about our vacation."

"Which is days after my birthday," Emmy said, smiling. "Bonus."

"Not as good as having you back," Bri said, lightly tapping her on the arm, to Emmy's surprise. "I've been worried you'd never act like yourself again."

"I second that," said Veren, winking at Brianna, who blushed a little.

Emmy glanced between them, then giggled a bit. "Well, I'm okay now, I guess." she said to both of them, then looked at Brianna. "And for future attempts, Bri, you hit just a little harder. Like this."

Brianna was pushed slightly by Emmy's demonstration, and she made a nervous sound. "It just seems like a weird gesture," she said.

"It is," Emmy agreed. "But it's just one of many ways friendship is expressed."

They walked in comfortable silence till they reached the bottom, then Veren faced them. "Alright, you two make sure everything's packed," he said. "I'll be away for a few hours, making sure we have plenty of food for the trip."

"What about water?" Bri asked, feeling a little thrill when Veren looked at her.

He chuckled, smiling. "Water is already taken care of," he said simply, then he ran off.

A few seconds later, Emmy counted off on her fingers. "Let's see" she mused. "With food and water taken care of, we just need clothes, towels, and swimsuits. Easy enough."

"Swimsuits?" Bri said, blinking several times. "What's that?"

Emmy looked at her, disbelieving. Then with a sigh, she took her wrist and pulled her along. "You'll see, Bri."

Brianna walked out of the school, dressed in her dull-black shirt and dark-blue skirt, chatting with Emmy as they walked out. Emmy was wearing her light-red top and light-blue skirt, and both of them carried a towel over their shoulders.

"I hope you'll enjoy your swimsuit, Bri," Emmy said, stretching her arms above her head.

"Well, we'll see about that," she said, feeling nervous. She wasn't entirely sure about showing this much of herself in front of her friends.

At the bottom of the steps, they found Veren, who was wearing his silver-gray t-shirt and gold shorts, a towel slung over his shoulder too. In his hands, he carried a large basket.

"All right, girls," he greeted easily, smiling softly. "Towels, check. Bathing suits?" he continued, tilting his head.

In answer, both girls simply moved their shirts a bit on the shoulders, revealing their straps. Brianna was a second slow in doing so, having been lost in her thoughts.

Veren nodded. "Check," he said, turning to lead the way. "We're all set."

And with that, they started walking off toward the city gate, and their mysterious destination.

"Okay girls, we're almost there," Veren said, climbing up this big hill. "Just fifty more feet."

Brianna climbed up the same path, Emmy following, at least until she heard her grunt. This prompted her to look back. "Emmy, are you okay?" she breathed, stepping closer.

Emmy sat on a big rock, taking off her right shoe and rubbing at her bare foot. "The long walk I can handle, but I've never walked this much over uneven terrain" she said, almost to herself. "And as a result, this nerve in the middle of my foot is throbbing."

Brianna put her hand on Emmy's shoulder, kneeling down. "If you can, try putting your weight on the back or sides of your foot," she said, knowing from experience, even though it had been years ago. "It takes some practice, but it helps with that nerve."

"Everything okay down there?" they heard, seeing Veren craning his neck, a good distance away.

"Yeah, we're fine!" Emmy called, standing up, testing Bri's advice.

In short order, they ran up the hill, pulling to a stop beside Veren. "There it is," he said simply, gesturing with a smile.

They both gasped as they saw where he was pointing.

Just below them, fifty feet away, was a small beach-like area. Two big trees overlooked the place, one on either side, their roots half-submerged in water. The river extended forward into the distance, eventually connecting to a much larger lake. In addition, they could see the outlines of the Hearts Mountains in the distance, directly in the middle of the lake. The light of the sun shone gently, filtering through the tree's leaves, giving the area a soft glow.

Emmy squealed, grinning brightly—the first time in a long while. "This place is beautiful! And so romantic!" she exclaimed.

Brianna blushed slightly at Emmy's use of the word *romantic*, but still smiled. "Yeah, it's amazing" she whispered in slight awe.

Veren grinned at his two friends, "Well? What did I tell you?" he said, chuckling slightly. "I told you this spot was special."

"Well, what are we waiting for here?" Emmy cried out, and within seconds, she was already running full speed toward the beach-like area. "Last one there's a rotten egg!" they heard as well.

Guess my advice is working for her she thought faintly, looking at Veren with a smile. But more than that, she was just glad to have her best friend back.

Veren simply laughed, and ran full speed after Emmy, Brianna following shortly behind him.

Emmy won the race because of her headstart, while Brianna and Veren were tied at last. After playfully teasing each other, they both figured it didn't matter who arrived last.

Emmy simply twirled in place, then turned to them with a grin. "Well? Let's go swimming!" she exclaimed, then quickly took off her shirt, revealing a light-pink halter top underneath. Getting rid of her other clothes, she revealed her bikini bottom in the process.

Veren blushed faintly at her act, not directly looking at her as she changed. Brianna was both faintly amused and embarrassed by Veren's reaction and Emmy's lack of modesty. Emmy pushed her pile of clothes just out of the way, then turned with a grin to them. "What are you two waiting for? Come on!"

Brianna slowly gulped silently, then began the process of taking off her own clothes. While she was doing so, Veren did the same—both trying not to look at each other. Still, Brianna couldn't help from looking at Veren's naked chest, but Veren did well not looking all the while.

By the end, Brianna was left in a dark-blue two-piece with a shirt length top that had a small silver symbol on the front. Next to her, Veren was left in a pair of red boardshorts, knee-length, with two small black symbols on the front.

By the time they finished, Emmy was already waist deep in the water. "Come on, you slowpokes! The water's great!" she called, then she fell over backward and the water with a *splash*! She came back up giggling, pushing her wet blonde hair out of her face.

Shaking his head with a knowing smile, Veren began to walk toward the water, Brianna following close behind. She tested it and recoiled, feeling a chill run up her toes.

"Oh! A little cold here," said Brianna, taking her time wading further in, while Veren was already waist-deep. Upon further inspection though, he was hiding the similar chill she was fighting.

Veren smiled at her, gently encouraging her further, "Come on, you can do it Bri."

She shook her head slightly, slowly taking a step further until she was within arms reach of Veren. "Not this fast, I can't."

Veren's smile slowly turned devious, "Well then, all you need is a little *pull*" he whispered deviously, making her blink and blush.

"Wait, what do you mean pull—Oh no, don't you dare—Ahh!" she said, changing her tone twice in mid-sentence.

Splash!

Quickly coming back up, she sputtered a bit. "Veren!" she exclaimed, seeing Veren chuckling with a big grin. After shaking excess water off her head, she smiled back. "You think you're funny, huh?" she said deviously. Then without warning she grabbed Veren's arm and pulled him down too.

"Ahh!" he cried out in surprise, falling into the water with a *splash*!

He quickly got back up with a grin. "Oh yeah?" he exclaimed, then he splashed some water into her face. She squealed in surprise, then she fought back with a grin, splashing water into his face. Thus, the splash war began, and continued for some time.

From farther away, Emmy simply laughed and shook her head. "Oh, the two lovebirds," she whispered sweetly, then she took in a breath and dove under the water.

Much later, the sun was close to setting, throwing long shadows across the trees. The three teenagers were sitting together on logs, just watching the sunset. Seconds passed, then Brianna felt her shoulder being tapped, and she looked over at Emmy, who was looking at her with a knowing smile.

"So, Bri—what are you gonna do about Veren?" she whispered discreetly, making sure Veren couldn't hear. Brianna made a small sound, glancing at Veren on her other side, some feet away. She turned back to Emmy to say something.

Emmy cut her off though/ "Seriously, Bri!" she whispered. "It's been six. Freaking. Months. Why haven't you done anything yet?"

Brianna stammered a bit, shaking her head as she tried to explain, only to be interrupted again/ "Oh, don't tell me you're still afraid!" she whispered disbelievingly.

"No!" she whispered discreetly. "No, I went through that awhile ago. Right now, I'm just uh, panicking that there's nothing left in the way". She blushed harder as she said it. "And while the six months passed, we were worried about your recovery."

Emmy made a sound, then smiled at her, placing a hand on her shoulder. "Okay then, Bri, just think of this" she whispered gently. "He likes you, and you like him."

She blushed brightly, glancing down at the ground. She knew that already, but it didn't stop the blush.

Emmy continued. "So you're only torturing yourselves by keeping it unsaid, especially since you could kiss," she whispered gently, with a bit of a tease. "Let me tell you what. I'm gonna go to bed now, and you will show your feelings tonight. If you don't, I'll kill you."

Brianna glanced up, giving Emmy an odd look.

Emmy smiled at her. "Not literally, of course. But still, you must do it tonight," she whispered, then she stretched and yawned audibly, getting Veren's attention and jolting Brianna.

I didn't think she'd do it this soon! she thought desperately.

"Well, I think I'm gonna go to bed now," Emmy said, smiling at them as she got up.

Veren nodded and smiled. "All right," he said.

With that, Emmy winked at Brianna then turned and walked away, leaving Brianna and Veren alone.

FIRST KISS

Veren slowly sighed, rubbing his head. "Oh man, I thought she'd *never* go to sleep," he whispered faintly, sounding relieved.

Brianna looked at him, completely surprised. "What?" she breathed.

Veren slowly looked at her, smiling sheepishly as he said, "Well, don't get me wrong. Emmy is a good friend, and I like her that way, but—" He blushed a bit as he glanced down. "It's more fun when it's just you and me," he whispered, blushing harder.

She looked down with a slightly embarrassed smile, a little numb at the thought this was actually happening. By instinct, her hand twitched a few times, then she slowly got it up and over Veren's shoulder. This surprised him, and he looked at her.

"I-I agree, Veren," she breathed, stammering slightly as she glanced at him, very nervous. "Emmy is my best friend, and I know she's yours too, in addition to me, but I like it better when you're the only one around," she whispered, looking down. "You're just more fun, really."

He slowly smiled, nudging her shoulder, much to her surprise. "Thanks for that, Bri."

Much to her relief, Veren slowly looked back at the sunset, and there was a comfortable silence between them. Her heart was pounding inside her chest despite her slow breathing. Unconsciously, she found her other hand fixing up her hair, trying to make herself look as good as possible. She didn't do anything to stop it, and she didn't want it to stop.

Breathing slowly, she slowly leaned her head down, resting it on Veren's right shoulder, making both of them blush. Veren didn't object though. He simply smiled at her then went back to watching the sunset.

Seconds passed, a faint breath of wind blowing at their hair. Feeling as if her heart were going to explode, she slowly looked up at him. The light of the sunset highlighted his hair, especially his bangs, only enhancing the soft look of his features.

At that exact instant, Veren's teachings on love ran through her head: the hand-holding, the hugging, and the kissing. She vividly remembered when he had shown her the "minor" kiss, but he hadn't the courage to do the "major" kiss. She remembered when she had seen Emmy doing it, she had been stunned.

Could she really do the same with Veren?

She looked down at Veren's hand and realized she was literally about a foot away from him. All it would take was one simple motion.

Before she knew it, her hand on his shoulder moved away, and then she smiled as she slowly took his right hand in hers, interlocking their fingers slowly.

Veren was startled, and he slowly looked directly at her.

Her initial reaction was panic; she'd meant to kiss him, not hold his hand! She immediately thought she ruined the moment, but she seemed frozen to the spot. And all the while, her heart felt as if it were going to explode.

Veren glanced down at their hands and made a small noise. "You beat me to it, Bri," he whispered faintly, in a daze.

"Huh?" she breathed, unable to process much else.

He didn't answer verbally; he sat closer and placed his hands on her shoulders, pulling her even closer.

She made a weak noise, all breath gone from her body, her heart way past exploding. Her face was all red. Breathing heavily, she literally felt her body heating up. She could feel Veren's breath on her lips.

Veren slowly leaned forward, his eyes slowly closing and his mouth opening slowly. She felt a thrill go up her spine, and she unconsciously did the same, feeling herself tremble a little.

After what seemed like an eternity, their lips connected.

Brianna trembled, feeling as if she were in heaven. Veren's soft lips kissing hers, the sense of closeness, and his hand on her cheek—it was just bliss. While she was kissing him back softly, her right hand slowly came up and rested on his cheek in return.

They couldn't get enough of each other, and they pulled each other closer as the kiss intensified. The only thing either one was aware of was each other, and they wanted more. The thrill intensified when Veren lightly sucked on her lips, hesitant and unsure.

From a distance away, on her makeshift bed, Emmy smiled as she saw them kissing. *Finally,* she snarked softly, turning away and laying down, closing her eyes.

April 18, 2028

Brianna stirred slowly, squinting as a bright light shone on her eyelids. But she wanted to stay there, snuggled against the warm ground.

Wait, the ground wasn't supposed to be warm, or this soft.

She half-opened her eyes, was briefly blinded, then found she was literally lying on the ground at an odd angle, with Veren underneath her.

She yelped and scrambled off him, kicking up a fair amount of dust and breathing heavily.

As she dusted off her clothes unconsciously, she glanced down at Veren, who's legs were sprawled over the log they'd sat on last night. And when she thought of last night, she felt her face grow warm, along with a rush of feelings. Once she finished dusting, she gently knelt down, trying to shake him. "Veren" she whispered gently.

It took many shakes, but eventually he was roused. *He sleeps like a rock* she thought, both happily and wryly.

Veren made a weak noise, then he got up, but he slipped and his head hit the log. "Ow!" he groaned, clutching his head with one hand.

"Veren!" she gasped, rushing to get him upright. "Are you okay?"

Veren staggered a bit once upright, but he steadied easily. "Yeah, I'm okay," he said, slowly removing his hand and looking at her. "Just a little bruise."

She made a little "ah" sound, holding him close, to his pleased surprise.

"Well, about time you two got up," they heard, seeing Emmy standing close by with a smile. "Thought you never would."

"Well, we have, as you see," Veren said lightly.

"Yeah, I saw" Emmy snarked with a smirk. "I saw everything."

She giggled as she walked off, leaving the couple blushing. But despite that, Bri asked, "Where are you going?"

"To get firewood," she replied, gesturing with one hand as she walked, not even looking back. "It's my turn to do that."

Minutes later, Emmy picked her way through the forest path, briefly jumping up on a log for fun.

Hmm, Bri's tip about keeping your weight on the back of your foot is really paying off. she thought, giggling slightly as she slowed a bit, lightly flexing her foot as the twigs and branches creaked underneath her. She could literally feel the difference when she walked, even though it took a little getting used to.

Then she looked around her, *Now, to find some firewood,* she thought.

Snap!

She whirled around in self-defense, but much to her relief, it was only a horse—wait a minute, how had a horse managed to sneak up on her, in the middle of a crunchy-sounding forest floor?

Then after the initial look, she stared at it.

The creature standing before her looked a lot like a horse; it had four legs, hooves at the end of each of them; long tail hair; a mane from it's long head. It's color was a slightly dull silvery white, with the tail and mane hair of a little darker shade. It must have been a tall breed, because it stood a least a foot taller than her at it's shoulder height. But the most eye-catching feature was the golden horn it sported, seamlessly attached to its head.

It regarded her with blue eyes. And judging by the way it nervously pawed the ground, it was just as surprised—and wary—as she had been.

"A unicorn?" she breathed, hardly daring to believe it; even seeing one of these was rare. "Whoa."

She couldn't believe her luck, but the moment she stepped forward, the unicorn snorted and seemed to tense. She froze, then slowly backed her foot to where it had been . . . the unicorn seemed to relax back to before, but it still didn't take it's eyes off her. She couldn't quite understand it.

Then a reflection of light off the tree beside the unicorn caught her attention, and she glanced in its direction.

She gasped; two little unicorns were hiding behind another tree, obviously frightened but even more curious about this stranger. One was golden colored and the other was blue, each of them about the size of an average dog. They didn't have horns just yet, but she could tell there were little stubs where they'd someday grow.

She had to try hard to keep herself from squealing; they were just plain adorable!

But she also realized with a jolt that those two little ones must be the children of the adult version regarding her. If she made one wrong move, this parent unicorn would justly trample her. Best thing to do was simply back away and get firewood somewhere else, but she hesitated. How often did people get to see unicorns, much less touch them?

Did she dare take that risk?

As she silently weighed the risks, the little blue unicorn backed up slightly, and part of his foot simply vanished.

She blinked, rubbed her eyes, and realized she had seem what she though she'd seen; part of the little one's foot had disappeared behind it. As she looked though—with the parent still watching her every movement—the little one must have been more curious, because it stepped forward—and the missing part of it's leg showed up again.

At first she was confused, but then it hit her—invisibility magic of some sort.

No *wonder* people didn't see them often! If they could use it on themselves, they could come and go as they pleased and no one would know!

She smiled softly, looking at the parent unicorn still watching her every move. Then she slowly sat down cross-legged on the forest floor.

Minutes passed as they stared at each other, then the parent unicorn slowly took a step toward her—then another, then another. Slowly but surely, he or she came toward her. But even when its nose was about two feet away, Emmy didn't reach out right away; she let this parent sniff her, to assure that she was no threat.

By some unspoken communication, the little ones wandered even closer, but they stayed a little distance away, just to be sure.

Emmy kept her eyes on the parent unicorn though, slowly raising her right hand a little, simply at first so he'd see it (she didn't know if it was a *he*, but it was easier to think of it as a *him*). Then she slowly raised her hand high, palm toward him, without getting up. He sniffed her hand then hesitantly pressed it against her hand.

His nose felt slightly wet, but she didn't mind. She smiled, gently stroking his nose, glad that she was this lucky.

She yelped a little when she felt a lick on her cheek, but it was only the little golden unicorn. *This little one's obviously the brave one,* she thought brightly, gently nuzzling her cheek against him.

She wanted to stand up, and she wanted to hug them all as they were just too adorable, but little steps at a time.

She heard a horse neigh somewhere nearby, startling her a bit. But obviously, the little ones knew what it meant. They hurried away from her (but the golden one sneaked another lick) while the parent gently removed himself from her hand. He followed his children, glancing behind at her as they disappeared through the invisibility barrier.

Despite knowing that she'd gotten farther than most, she was still disappointed that it had to end. She slowly sighed, then got herself off the ground, brushing her hands against her butt.

"Bye-bye, my friends" she said gently to the wind. "Maybe I'll call the big one Charlie. Charlie the unicorn."

She giggled a little, already faintly cheered. Then she turned around and saw what she could do with the log she had stepped over; she still had a job to do.

But boy, would she have a tale to tell around the campfire!

At around the same time, Keith sat in his office, passing away the time with a random drawing. He chuckled to himself, looking at the scribbled thing; he couldn't draw to save his life, but he had nothing better to do.

Luckily, there was a knock on his door. "Come in," he said automatically, putting the paper away.

One of his many hired messengers came in, giving a short bow. But one detail in particular from this teenager caught Keith's eye.

"So you got a blue streak in your hair now?" he asked plainly.

"Yes, sir" he said, with a hint of teenage stubbornness. "Is that a problem?"

Keith took a moment to think. He knew from several exchanges that this particular kid—he couldn't recall his name at the moment—was at the height of his rebellious phase, even for a teenager. Saying that he hated it would only delight him, even as he reacted with arguments and words he'd regret later. But neither should he say outright it's the greatest thing ever, or he might just think so himself.

And the one detail he'd never mention out loud was that he actually kind of liked the look.

"Well," he mused. "right now, I don't really hate it, or love it. I don't know. I can't tell if it's working for you or not"

The teen struggled not to react, but Keith saw his words hit home, though any lasting effects were ambiguous. Finally, the teen raised his head stiffly. "You want the reports, sir?"

"Yes, I do."

"The intelligence service's efforts to find the woman responsible," he started, at attention, though in a loose sense, "Still negative."

He hummed thoughtfully. "She must be very skilled to hide that well for this long."

"Or they're just incompetent," the teen muttered under his breath, but loud enough for Keith to hear.

He ignored it. "And?"

"The number of Oathkeepers is growing every day," he continued. "They've now got enough to patrol the center of the city. However, they still estimate many months before they get enough to patrol the whole city efficiently."

Months huh? Keith thought to himself, wincing a bit on behalf of Bri, Emmy and Veren. He was sure they could handle it, but it would really tax them. Shame he couldn't help their boredom himself.

Next, the teen listed off several things that weren't really important to the overall plot, just how to run a school. This included the weekly repair crews, water treatment and restocking on food.

"Twenty percent off for the week, hmm?" Keith asked, then chuckled. "Very well, tell Mrs. Harrell that I'll take her up on her offer"

He nodded, then turned and let himself out, Keith watching the door for several moments, then he sighed.

For roughly six months, things had been in a peaceful lull, but the mention of the woman still out there brought back a sobering fact: this wasn't over yet. And now, he couldn't shake the feeling that things were going to happen. But when would that be? Soon, not so soon, even a few more months?

He rubbed his temple, sighing again; the wait was the most maddening part.

VACATION INTERRUPTED

June 6, 2028

Brianna breathed slowly, standing at her post on the outer wall. She slowly smiled as her thoughts wandered.

It had been a good vacation, what with Veren and her finally together, and Emmy's surprise encounter with unicorns, and of course the actual relaxing part. Now they were back at "work", but thinking back to those moments made her feel tingly inside. Or was it simply warm?

Suddenly, she was lifted off her feet from behind, making her gasp in surprise. "Having fun?" a voice whispered in her ear.

Giggling profusely, she twisted around in Veren's arms and kissed him, which he returned in kind. They continued for a good while, not noticing anything else.

"Get a room," came the playful snark, startling them both as they pulled apart.

Emmy giggled herself, stepping in between them with a knowing smirk.

They both tried to explain, but Emmy stopped them with a raised hand. "Don't bother, you two lovebirds," she said, giggling at them, then smiling as she tilted her head. "So what are we gonna do for our next upcoming vacation? Which, by the way, is extra sweet for only being two months apart this time."

There was silence for a few seconds as they thought about it, then Veren spoke up. "Well, we can go camping again," he said, smiling. "After all, you all enjoyed my secret place."

"That sounds good to me," Emmy said with a smile, then tilted her head at Bri. "What about you, Bri?"

Bri felt herself grow giddy that they'd be returning to Veren's secret spot. "Sure," she said, slowly nodding. "That would be fine. Just don't forget my birthday."

They both laughed, saying they wouldn't think of it. But their celebration was cut short by a familiar half-hissing, half-sizzling sound.

Bri instantly turned around, feeling her heart pound. *Calm down, just remember Veren's idea,* she forcibly thought to herself.

Emmy looked out over the wall then breathed out. "They're very far down, but they're coming up fast," she said, bringing up one foot. "Let's get moving."

"Yay," Veren breathed halfheartedly, not looking forward to it, but he applied the magic to his feet all the same.

Bri finished doing so, then carefully walked up to the stone's edge, then promptly "walked" from an upright, standing position to a ninety degree angle on the wall. She could already see Oblivions running up the wall, and her hands clenched, but she forced herself to breath. *Focus* she thought, recalling Setxis's face.

She saw it; Oblivions continued to run up the wall, but each one had an image of Setxis superimposed over them, each doing a different thing (and one of which was considerably rude).

She ran down toward them.

One hissed and attempted to cut her in half, but she did the same before it could. Two others fell just the same, then she came across a fourth one, and she raised her warpblade to kill it.

The Oblivion hissed, then her image of Setxis changed into James, confused, blinking, not knowing where he was or who he was.

She gasped, and only sheer luck saved her as the creature's claws scratched her cheek. She cried out from the sudden pain, but she quickly stabbed the Oblivion, her other hand holding her cheek. Luckily, she didn't seem to be bleeding, but maybe that was simply because of her hand. *What the hell just happened?* she thought, utterly confused.

Another attempted to hit her from behind, but she dodged, and the battle resumed.

She managed to deal with her group just the same, but she remained worried as she slowly got back up on the wall. Panting a bit, she held her cheek as her hand glowed green, healing herself slowly.

What happened down there? she thought weakly, looking around; Emmy and Veren were similarly resting from the battle, and she'd been the last to deal with her group. "Veren?"

He was surprised, but he got up with a small groan. "Yeah?" he asked, standing two feet away.

"I think something's wrong," she whispered, worried. "Your tip with dealing with the Oblivions—I saw Setxis's face for the first few, but then it changed into James! And no matter what I tried down there, I kept seeing his face, and I couldn't bring myself to attack him."

"Oh man" Veren said, groaning and rubbing a hand along his temple. "I really thought that was a good idea for you," he added, sounding disappointed.

"But this is normal, right?" she insisted. "Right?"

"Yeah, of course it is," he said quickly, looking at her. "Despite what "Setxis" has done, James had no hand in it. I perfectly understand why you couldn't bring yourself to hurt him, even if he was just an image in your head."

She breathed out in relief then hugged him. "Thank you."

She couldn't see his smile, but she knew it was there as he held her back. "Anytime," he whispered gently.

She enjoyed being in his grip, just feeling warm, but she slowly noticed she was feeling another warm sensation—somewhere between her legs.

She barely avoided turning red. Her period. If Veren found this was happening right now, that'd be so embarrassing!

Well—at least I won't have to worry about it happening on our vacation, she thought, feebly chuckling inside her head.

June 9, 2028

"Well, we've arrived girls," Veren exclaimed, looking out over his secret spot as the sun was high in the sky.

Brianna smiled as she looked at it herself, but inside she couldn't stop feeling giddy. *Where we first kissed,* she thought happily.

Beside her, Emmy seemed to notice her general thoughts, but she only smiled. "Well, come on, you two! Let's have fun!" she yelled, already racing full speed toward the lake like last time.

Brianna chuckled at the same time as Veren did, and they slowly made their way down to the lake at their own pace.

"Man, you two sure took your time!" Emmy called out, giggling playfully as Brianna and Veren walked into the secret spot hand in hand.

Veren simply looked at Brianna, smiling as he shook his head. "Don't mind her. Let's just have fun like we planned," he said, getting a smile out of her as she nodded.

"Agreed," she said, squeezing his hand softly. He smiled back, then they slowly made their way closer to the middle of the secret spot.

As soon as they got there, Veren went over to search for big stones, which they would use for their makeshift campfire. Brianna carefully dug a small pit with her feet, arranging the logs from their last trip into place afterward.

Emmy soon helped with that, both of them straining from the effort. Brianna slowly sat down, her bathing suit under her clothes. "Emmy?" she whispered softly, just as Emmy was about to turn.

Emmy looked at her, head tilted with a smile. "Yes, Bri?"

Brianna sighed faintly, feeling slightly uneasy now. "Well, you see, I'm a bit nervous here about something" she started, not sure how to say it.

"About love?" she asked gently, sitting down beside her, her smile soft. "You two are so happy. Why are you nervous?"

Brianna breathed in and out faintly, glancing up at her. "Well, look at how I've been acting," she whispered in a small rush. "Happy all the time, energetic, excited—kinda like you" she continued, then glanced down. "It's not like me."

"True," Emmy agreed, nodding with a teasing giggle. "But don't worry, *every* couple goes through this first stage—the happiness stage."

Brianna blinked slowly, glancing up at Emmy. "So, I'll be back to normal soon?" she whispered, slowly smiling. "I won't become a different person?"

Emmy laughed, her chest heaving a little. "Not by a long shot," she giggled, grinning. "You may be a little out-of-character now, but you're still the same Bri underneath, and you don't need to worry about that."

Brianna breathed out in relief, leaning back a bit and smiling. "Well—that's great news" she murmured faintly. "I was afraid I had gone a little crazy there, acting like I have been lately, but now I know it's natural."

"It is," Emmy said, smiling gently, then she touched her hand to her shoulder, surprising Brianna. "But," Emmy started, faintly serious now, "let me tell you, the happiness stage will end, and then—the real challenge begins."

Brianna blinked in surprise, but before she could ask, Emmy continued.

"Anyone can be in love, but once you start getting to know each other—every detail, every quirk, every behavior—things may change," Emmy whispered faintly, then tilted her head. "If you're not similar at all, things won't end well. If you are though, you could potentially go beyond being a couple."

"Beyond?" Brianna murmured slowly, confused. "There's beyond being a couple?"

Emmy blushed faintly, chuckling as she bumped her shoulder with Brianna's, standing up. "That's for another time, Bri," she whispered gently.

"Hey, girls, I'm back," a voice grunted from their right. It was Veren, and he was carrying about ten stones. The weight wasn't really the issue; it was the awkward arrangement he was barely managing. "Mind giving me a hand?"

"Sure," Emmy agreed, quickly moving over and taking five stones. Veren sighed in relief, slowly placing his pile near the ground they would use for their campfire.

Brianna stood up to help, but then she froze in shock.

About ten feet away, a swirling black vortex had appeared on the ground. It swirled faster and faster, then suddenly, a pair of paws dug itself out of the ground. The claws dug in deeper, then out jumped a dark-blue blur, landing on all four paws.

Brianna blinked several times, then her eyes lit up. "Fenrir!" she cried out, quickly running forward and burying her face into his fur. Fenrir growled low in pleasure, crouching down on his legs to allow her easier access. They stayed this way for several seconds, Brianna enjoying the feel of his fur.

She pulled away slightly, looking up into his yellow eye with a smile. "It's been too long, Fenrir," she whispered happily, smiling up at him. "Again."

He growled slightly in agreement, rubbing his head against her. She stepped back slightly, smiling as she glanced around. Veren simply smiled at them, dropping another large stone into the pit she had dug. "It's nice to see you again, Fenrir," he called, adjusting the stones a bit. Fenrir nodded his head to him, but his eyes strayed as Emmy quickly ran up to them.

"Oh, Fenrir's joining our days of fun, is he?" she said excitedly.

"Uh, I'm not sure he's joining the fun. He only just got here," Veren called, looking up briefly from his stone adjusting.

"Well, I hope he stays," said Emmy with a faint pout, then she looked up at Fenrir. "Are you?"

For awhile, at least, he broadcasted his thoughts, startling them slightly, but only because it was unexpected. *I have some time to be with you three.*

Brianna giggled softly, walking toward the logs they had arranged around the pit. Fenrir followed behind her slowly. "So tell me, Fenrir," she said, sitting down comfortably, looking up at him. "Why the delay between your visits?" she asked, tilting her head.

Curled around the log, a small black tendril extended outward from his head to hers, softly connecting to her forehead. As he did so, Emmy and Veren sat down on their opposite logs.

I'm sorry I couldn't appear more, said Fenrir inside her mind. *but things have become difficult for my kind.*

Strangely, Brianna's mouth opened with every word he spoke, surprising them all as Fenrir spoke through Brianna. It was very involuntary.

Veren glanced at Emmy. "That's new," he whispered discreetly, Emmy nodding.

Brianna blinked, looking up at Fenrir. "But why? I thought your kind could take care of themselves," she said aloud, so both Fenrir and her friends could hear.

Fenrir breathed slowly. *We can, but something is affecting the world* he said. *Something strong and unnatural—It's casting it's dark influence everywhere, and things are changing.*

Brianna tilted her head up at him. "Do you know what it is?" she asked. "And how is it affecting the world?"

Fenrir almost seemed to sigh. *I do not have proof, but I suspect the Oblivions,* he said. *Those abominations are not natural creatures. They were created by something, or someone.*

Brianna rubbed her head slightly, "I kinda thought so," she said. "Nature sure didn't seem to create those things."

And second, thought Fenrir, who closed his yellow eyes. *The dark influence I've spoken of, I've felt it ever since those Oblivions showed up. It's affecting the brains of creatures everywhere, nudging them to violent emotions and actions. Even my own kind.*

Brianna looked up at Fenrir with sad eyes, feeling through their connection his shame at this turn of events. She leaned against his soft dark-blue fur, wishing she could help in some way. "That's awful," she whispered to him. "How are you dealing with it?"

Fenrir slowly opened his yellow eyes again as he curled around the log. *I'm not sure about the other creatures, but my kind is resistant to this dark influence, thanks to our experience with dark powers. Many of us are capable of ignoring it, but there are a few who—think otherwise. I've been urging my kind and my pack to use our darkness powers to help slow down this dark influence. So far, it's going well, but I am at a loss to understand why you humans aren't affected.*

"Maybe because we aren't being targeted," Veren said thoughtfully, having finished with the stones. "If this influence is really that vast, we should be affected as well, but we're not."

Emmy touched a finger to her mouth. "That's really good, Veren. But why not target us?"

"I don't think any of us knows why," Bri answered, lightly playing with a few stray fur hairs. "Not yet. Fenrir's only just told us after all."

"Like I said," Veren added, causing them to look at each other and blush a little.

"Wait a minute," Emmy said slowly in realization. "Fenrir, did you say 'my pack' earlier?"

Fenrir's eyes moved slightly, but the three of them couldn't place what it meant. *Yes,* he answered. *I'm the alpha of my own pack. Did you expect anything less?*

After shaking off the surprise that overcame the three of them (which took some time), Bri managed to shake her head. "Not really, it just took us by surprise," she said. "I mean, you never gave any hints before."

Fenrir made a low sound in his throat, which Brianna translated as laughter. *Well, perhaps I did—*

Fenrir stiffened and stood up, his ears upright. Cautiously moving forward, he sniffed the air as he approached the water's edge. He snarled as he crouched backward, seemingly waiting for something. Seconds passed with only the wind moving. All three teenagers were a little tense themselves; they knew something was up.

The water erupted outward, splashing everything within fifty feet. All three of them cried out in surprise and shock, instinctively covering their heads as the water drenched them. Fenrir didn't move a muscle, even as he got soaked, continuing to glare at the source of the eruption. All throughout this, there was a low, venomous hiss in the air.

The three teens slowly recovered, flicking themselves as dry as they could. They slowly looked up at the source and pretty much froze in shock.

The thing staring down at them was a giant golden sea serpent. It was covered from head to tail in overlapping scales, which seemed to glow from the sunlight. It was at least forty-five feet tall, its bright green eyes narrowed at them in a hungry manner. The two fangs it sported were monstrous, extending past its lower jaw like a sabertooth's, including rows of razor sharp teeth. Occasionally, two forked tongues would sneak into the open.

Fenrir got a running start and jumped up high, aiming for the serpent's throat. At the same time, the sea serpent lunged hard and fast at Fenrir.

The sea serpent missed, grazing its head against the ground, while Fenrir overshot his jump, landing far back on his scaly form. The sea serpent hissed in outrage and turned after Fenrir. Fenrir ran and jumped the length of the sea serpent, twisting his enemy every which way, almost as if trying to tie it in a knot.

Unfortunately, this never happened. The sea serpent seemed to be aware of that tactic.

The sea serpent opened its mouth wide, spewing a stream of icicles at Fenrir. Fenrir jumped off part of its back, narrowly missing the incoming missiles, which shattered against the serpent's scales without effect. Fenrir landed on another part of the serpent's back, then instantly changed direction and jumped right at his mouth.

The sea serpent merely hissed, then *head-butted* Fenrir.

He went flying through the water—like a skipping stone at first, then straight through a section as he were a boat. He finally stopped at the shallow end, shaking his wet fur as he stood up. He growled loudly as he faced the sea serpent again, whose mouth was wide open with small shimmers.

Fenrir tried to jump, only to find out the water around his paws had frozen solid.

The sea serpent sprayed Fenrir with literally freezing breath, the swirling cold and ice concealing him from view.

After ten seconds of this, the sea serpent stopped, and the swirling ice started to disperse. A swirling black shield whirled around where Fenrir had been. Then the sea serpent, hissing in anticipation, moved closer before it disappeared.

But Fenrir had disappeared—only the ice remained where his paws had been.

The sea serpent narrowed its eyes, only for a purple-black tendril to whip it across the head. Hissing, it brought it's attention to the source: Fenrir on one of the land pieces framing the beach, facing the sea serpent with fangs bared. The purple-black tendril-whip was connected right to his tail, with a similar glow coming from his claws.

Growling, Fenrir let his tendril-whip snake through the air at tremendous speed, right at the serpent's throat. The sea serpent hissed and effortlessly dodged, then on the second time, managed to clamp down on the tendril whip, prompting a frustrated growl. Then with a mighty yank, it pulled Fenrir high into the air.

Fenrir flailed a bit as he flew, but quickly managed to angle himself straight at the sea serpent's head. It opened its mouth unnaturally wide, ready to down him in one gulp.

It was not that easy; Fenrir landed directly on it's right fang—the impact staggered it—even as Fenrir ran up and tried to claw out the serpent's eyes. He merely glanced off the protective membranes, while the sea serpent shook Fenrir off, making him fly again. By the looks of it, Fenrir's second landing was just as smooth as his last one.

The sea serpent shot its freezing breath at Fenrir again, much larger this time.

Seconds passed as the sea serpent spewed its freezing breath, then a purple-black force field expanded rapidly, pushing the cold and ice elements outward fast. It burst open like an explosion, stopping the sea serpent as it hissed, glaring.

Fenrir met this gaze with a growl, fangs bared. A "bring it on," if they'd ever seen one.

At the same time, Fenrir's tail became coated with darkness, extending far beyond its normal length. The sea serpent hissed and lunged forward, but Fenrir's darkness-coated tail lunged forward even faster.

He slammed his opponent in the head, stopping it cold. Before the sea serpent could recover, he slammed it again, sending it reeling backward. A third attack smashed him against the opposite land piece with a *crash*!

Fenrir simply watched the sea serpent struggling as his darkness-coated tail retracted to normal length, the darkness dissipating completely.

The sea serpent slowly got its bearings back, then hissed venomously, lunging forward with a murderous glare. Whiplash slammed the sea serpent back against the cliff, sending small pieces of rubble outward. The sea serpent blinked in confusion then struggled hard against the cliff. No matter how much it struggled though, it couldn't move forward at all, or too much to the left or right. Fenrir simply watched the sea serpent struggle futilely, his claws still glowing purple-black.

As it struggled, it became clear that the sea serpent was ensnared by it's own shadow.

Fenrir then took a solid stance and opened his mouth slightly, the inside glowing purple-black. The loose material around Fenrir began shaking slightly.

Fenrir reared his head, then more-or-less roared.

A massive beam of pure darkness shot out, soaring across the space in front of him. The sea serpent barely had enough time for its pupils to shrink inward.

Boom!

The sea serpent slammed against the cliff then started falling with a wounded hiss. It fell with a loud crash near the three teenagers, making them jump with shock; they'd been too busy watching to react much.

The golden sea serpent lay there with it's head on the beach, completely out cold. Traveling by the shadows again, Fenrir appeared by the serpent's side in seconds, getting up on its scaly neck. Fenrir moved forward slowly, sniffing the sea serpent's unmoving body carefully.

Brianna stared at Fenrir, along with Emmy and Veren. Hey, how many times did you see a fight between a Fenrir and a giant sea serpent?

Fenrir glanced over at them, then turned away from them, slowing once he reached the water's edge. And even from a distance, they could tell he was breathing heavily and was a little unsteady with his walk.

Then he projected with his thoughts, *The sea serpent is still alive, but you don't have to worry. My pack will feast on it's meat.*

Brianna blinked in surprise, and a glance around showed that Veren and Emmy felt much the same.

By the water's edge, Fenrir lowered his head a bit then howled to the sky.

It was a beautiful sound, and it echoed long into the day. Brianna thought she had never heard a more lovely and haunting sound in her life; she wished she could listen to it forever. After about ten seconds, Fenrir's howling trailed off, then he stood there, waiting.

They didn't have to wait long.

A low hum sounded nearby, startling Brianna and the others as they whirled around. A few feet away from them, three separate darkness vortexes had appeared. They swirled faster and faster, then in the space of a second, three pairs of claws appeared, and out leapt three blurs—all three landing near Fenrir.

Brianna saw out of the corner of her eye Fenrir making an effort to straighten up, to not show weakness. But for the most part, she was far more fascinated with the newcomers, as were Emmy and Veren.

The three newcomers were Fenrirs, two slightly smaller than the one they knew, and one larger but not bulky. The only notable difference was the color, and all three were different colors: one was somewhere between pure and dull black, another was a dark gold, and the other was a silver gray. The two smaller ones seemed to be female as their tales and manes were less puffed out. They had the same yellow eyes, though there were different shades between the four of them.

The three of them started conversing with Fenrir—a cascade of barks, growls and other sounds—but he seemed to understand it all. Fenrir growled back, responding to what they had said. Despite the fact that the dark tendril had been disconnected, Brianna's mind got a few insights into what he was saying,—*discuss this—later. For now—this serpent back—a meal.*

She found that really weird and wondered how that worked.

The three Fenrirs growled slightly in agreement, but they did glance back at Brianna, Emmy, and Veren for a moment. Then, the three of them moved quickly, their paws beginning to glow.

Purple-black energy spread outward from all three of them, covering the entire unconscious sea serpent. A second later, the sea serpent itself began to sink into the swirling energy, disappearing bit by bit from their sight. Eventually, it was gone.

With a final glance back, all three Fenrirs turned and ran, jumping into the swirling energy vortex. A few seconds later, the vortex disappeared entirely.

Fenrir relaxed just the slightest, then turned and settled himself in front of them, licking at a part of himself they couldn't see. Now relatively up-close, they could see he'd been scratched up pretty bad, due to his "skidding" incidents in the water.

Bri slowly ran a hand over his fur, worried for him. Before she could ask if she could heal him though, Veren spoke up, "Uh, Fenrir? Why did they look at us like that?"

"And do you fight those things on a regular basis?" Emmy also asked, sounding impressed.

Fenrir's licking didn't pause. *Once every so often, we like a challenge,* he projected with his thoughts. *But because we haven't gotten any prey this last week, that wasn't an option. We didn't have time for a long fight. My pack was hungry, so I had to make quick work of it. And also—they don't exactly understand my affection toward you three.*

Brianna blushed slightly from that last part. "But why?" she asked, curious.

They just don't understand why, that's all he thought to her, a yellow eye glancing right at her. *They don't know much about humans in general, and most of them are skeptical about what I tell them.*

"But they still respect you, right?" she asked.

Fenrir's eyes glinted. *Of course, I've proven how powerful I am time and time again. Most of them just consider my affection for you as a small quirk and don't really mind all that much.*

Brianna smiled at that statement. "I'm glad."

Fenrir slowly went closer and curled his fur against Brianna. *But sadly, there are other matters I must attend to. I don't know when I'll be able to visit again*

Brianna curled against his fur, holding as much as she could. "I understand," she said sadly, but with understanding. "I'll miss you, Fenrir."

Fenrir slowly stood up next to her, looking down at them with his yellow eyes. *And I'll miss you too, Brianna. You and your friends.*

With that, Fenrir turned and opened up his own swirling vortex. After another glance at them, he leapt into it, and the vortex disappeared seconds afterward.

June 11, 2028

Brianna sighed as she sat there on a log, looking down slightly, one hand holding up her chin. It was quiet at the campsite, with Emmy gathering firewood for the night, and Veren sitting high up in a tree.

She continued to sit there, only making the slightest acknowledgment when Emmy announced she was back. When Emmy sat down beside her, it jolted her a bit. "Where's Veren?"

"Up there," she said faintly, pointing without looking.

She didn't see Emmy look up, but she did see her lean down to get into her vision, eyebrows furrowed. "What happened?" she breathed. "This really isn't like you."

"I'm just sad," she said, looking up faintly. "And confused."

"About what?"

"Well," she started, fidgeting on the spot. "It started with us kissing, and I didn't notice anything else, until Veren cried out in pain. As I soon figured out, I had accidentally bit his tongue."

"Ouch," Emmy rasped, flinching a bit. "Is he okay?"

"By now, I think he is," she whispered. "But there was a bit of blood at the time,"

"Then what happened?"

"Well, he said some things. It got me mad and then it became a fight," she said sadly, looking down. "I realize now he only said those things because of his pain, but it still hurt. And I don't know what to do now."

Emmy sighed, placing a hand on her friend's shoulder. "Yeah, I know," she said sadly. "When Veren's in pain, he tends to throw nice out the window."

"And I'm conflicted," Brianna said, still looking down. "I don't know whether to apologize first for biting his tongue, as I tried to earlier, or if I should wait for him to apologize first for saying those things."

Emmy was silent for awhile, then she smiled slightly. "Your first fight," she said simply.

Brianna blinked several times, slowly looking up at Emmy. "What?" she said weakly.

"Your first fight," she repeated. "You've gone through the happy phase—a very long and drawn-out one—and now you've gotten your first fight. You've come a long way from when we first met you, Bri."

Brianna looked at her for a few seconds, then she sighed. "I don't really think having my first fight is something to celebrate, Emmy," she whispered faintly.

"It is when it's part of a larger character development, Bri," she said sweetly, pulling her closer to her. In fact, she pulled hard enough that Brianna's head landed on Emmy's shoulder, which made her blink in surprise.

"Uh," she said, slowly lifting her head back to normal, not sure what to say, "thanks."

Emmy nodded, smiling. "But seriously," she said, tilting her head, "one little fight won't ruin things. You love each other, so you'll come around, even if it takes some time."

Brianna glanced upward a little, considering things.

Veren sighed, sitting up on a high branch of the tree.

The few times he was here, it usually relaxed him to be on this spot, just looking out at the beach and the waves and feeling the wind on his face. But right now, he couldn't admire the view, not with what was going on his head. He couldn't get it out of his head, what he'd said to Bri—and what she'd said to him.

What the hell!? What are you trying to do, make me bleed to death?

It was an accident!

Oh yeah? Well maybe if you watched where you rubbed your teeth—

You're the one who moved too quickly, startling me and making me bite down by instinct!

And similar things. he thought faintly, hitting his head once against the wood with a sigh. *Still, I really think it's my fault. I'm the one who made a wrong move, and made her bite down by instinct. I was just an idiot to yell at her, especially since she tried to help.*

Why should he apologize though? She'd been the one to rub her teeth the wrong way in the first place, making him flinch slightly and causing her to bite down.

He growled slightly, rubbing his fingers along his temple. *More darkness-influenced thoughts. Great,* he thought sarcastically.

Still, he knew that the darkness only enhanced what was already there. On some level, he did feel that Bri should be the one to apologize since she'd made the first wrong move—rubbing her teeth. But he also knew it would be idiotic of him to say that and leave both of them hesitant and conflicted for a good while. He had no desire to continue that, so he knew he had to do the right thing and apologize.

His dark thoughts wouldn't let it be that easy though; he knew by experience.

The sun was half-hidden by the horizon, the sky slowly darkening as the sun disappeared.

Brianna sat on the log, looking into the fire. Veren sat beside her. Unlike most times though, there was space between them, and the mood was completely awkward. Emmy sat across them on another log, glancing at them as she adjusted the fire carefully.

What should I do? Brianna thought to herself, glancing at Veren's hands briefly, which lay at his sides. *It's clear he's no longer angry or in pain, but I still don't know if I should apologize first or not. But still, this fight is becoming torture.*

She wanted to say she was sorry, and she did want him to say he was sorry. She just wasn't sure about the timing or what Veren was feeling. She kicked herself mentally for that last one; she'd been so enthralled by the happiness that she hadn't paying much attention lately.

Eventually, she just turned toward Veren. The problem was, he had done so as well, and they spoke at the exact same time:

"I'm sorry! I was just mad, and I didn't mean what I said!"

"I'm sorry! I was mad at what you said, and I didn't mean to fight!"

Both of them blinked then stared at each other. Then they both blushed a little, slowly turning back to the fire, completely silent. Neither of them had heard what the other had said.

Across them, Emmy sighed silently, shaking her head a little. *Well, it's a start,* she thought wryly, adjusting the fire again as the sky darkened. *They'll come around though.*

The sun disappeared, the night sky turning black.

"Uh, guys?" said Emmy, her voice going slack.

"What?" Veren said, looking up at Emmy. Emmy pointed, and all three of them looked up at the Hearts Mountains, where she was pointing. At first they saw nothing in the faint light, but then they did.

An advancing wall of darkness swiftly moved down the central mountain—and in their direction.

"What is that!?" Brianna exclaimed, standing up immediately with Veren following her lead.

"I'll find out," came the serious answer, making Brianna glance over at Emmy. "I hope this works," Emmy said, this time to herself.

All ten of Emmy's fingertips were glowing green, and she slowly applied them to her closed eyes. Gradually, the magic sank into her eyes as she breathed slowly.

After a second or two, she opened her eyes. The green of her eyes now glowed by themselves, which was disorienting to look at. Emmy blinked tentatively, adjusting to whatever she had done.

"What did you do to your eyes?" Brianna whispered quietly, hoping not to disrupt anything.

Emmy slowly looked up at the advancing wall of darkness. "I enhanced my vision," Emmy whispered, her eyes moving very slowly, with careful focus.

Emmy's eyes slowly narrowed, then they widened in horror. "It's Oblivions! Thousands of them! Coming straight for us!" she yelled, eliciting similar reactions from Brianna and Veren.

Emmy quickly rubbed her eyes hard, returning them to normal. "We gotta get outta here!" she yelled, and the three of them scattered. "Pack up, quick!"

FIGHT OF THEIR LIVES

The three of them ran toward Liark as fast as they could. Brianna mentally called out for Fenrir several times, but there was no answer. She was really worried now, and her old fear was rising once again. The Oblivion army followed close behind them.

It was no use though; they couldn't run forever, and they slowed as they got tired. Then they were surrounded by the Oblivions. It was a sea of black, but with glowing dark-yellow eyes and lines of dark blue everywhere.

Brianna literally began shaking, and back-to-back-to-back as they were, the others felt it. "Bri, relax," Veren said, his voice tense. "Remember what I taught you."

"I-I can't!" she rasped, struggling to breathe in her panic. "T-There's so many of them!"

"She's right, Veren," Emmy whispered, her breathing heavy. "Their numbers aren't hundreds, they're thousands!"

"Damn it!" Veren cursed, raising his warpblade high. "Damn them all!"

With that, he charged straight forward, destroying three in a single blow.

This enraged the Oblivions, and they surged forward with hisses. Brianna barely ducked under a claw attack, and pretty soon, the adrenaline began to overtake her fear. With a small snarl, she sent a fireball into their midst. Five evaporated, several staggered from the fire clinging to them, and more replaced them.

Okay then, she thought grimly, her body glowing faintly, then she gripped both her warpblades. Since she was wearing normal clothes, it wasn't obvious which drive she was in, except for her abilities.

She ran forward, slashing left-and-right, then spin-kicked five of them across the field. She jumped high to avoid claw attacks, a few following her into the air. She twisted, then destroyed them with a vertical-spin attack. Tendrils grabbed her by both arms, pulling her back to the ground hard.

Groaning a bit, she found she was still bound by the tendrils. Growling, she gripped those tendrils and swung them around, slamming the connected Oblivions into many of their kind.

She twisted around; another Oblivion had sneaked up below her and grabbed her by the arm.

"Get off me!" she snarled, then she grabbed it by the chest with her other hand and slammed it over her head into the ground. She stabbed it, and the Oblivion evaporated with a hiss. She clutched her head, her courage drive fading and draining her mental endurance a bit.

Shaking it off, she looked up and saw even more surrounding her. The fear briefly resurged, but she forced it down. It wasn't easy though, so she focused on getting into a stance, ready to take on more of them.

And they answered her challenge.

They kept coming in endless waves, and she kept on fighting, time itself a blur as she hacked and slashed. Her muscles ached, and her headache got worse with every use of magic and drive, but she kept fighting. Finally, her leg seized up and she fell down on one knee, crying out at the pain. Breathing heavily, she fully expected to be attacked at that moment.

When five seconds passed and she wasn't attached, she was stunned in the back of her mind.

She looked up, still breathing heavily as she recovered. The Oblivion's were still an endless wave, and they surrounded her. But at her very weakest moment, they weren't attacking her.

What? she thought weakly, clutching at her side. *What's wrong with them?*

When she recovered enough, she glowed again, this time in her quick drive.

Moving in a blur, she skated across the ground, destroying Oblivion's everywhere she looked. But despite that, something was wrong: she was off-balance at critical moments, her attacks had slowed down to the point where some Oblivions could block her attacks, and her form was off.

What's happening? she thought weakly, slashing through a few Oblivions behind her. *I know I'm exhausted, but this isn't exhaustion. What is it?*

As she blocked an Oblivion's claw, her thoughts inexplicably went to her days of guarding the city, the majority of which had been spent on the outer wall. Just when she wondered why, it hit her: because of their job, they'd only gotten occasional combat experience. Before that, they had been training virtually every day.

We've gotten sloppy, all three of us she realized in dawning horror. *And it's working against us at the worst possible time!*

Not minutes later, or so she thought, she brought herself out of her quick drive. She groaned heavily at the headache, which nearly made her black out. *This isn't good* she thought weakly, breathing heavily as it brought her to the ground. *I can't keep going on like this. It'll destroy me.*

For a few moments, she looked across the sea of Oblivions, feeling a little numb inside. Once again, they did not attack her at her weakest moments, simply stared her unnervingly. She couldn't understand it.

But—I can't give up!

So, not a minute later, she wearily dragged herself off the ground, and glowed again.

As her muscles ached even worse and her vision began to blur at the edges, she fought on, losing her ability to breathe effectively. Despite that, gaps began to appear in the sea of Oblivions.

For the umpteenth time, she fell onto the ground, clutching at her side as she heaved. Somewhere during her heaves, she coughed fiercely and her vision blackened quite a bit. As her eyes closed, her hand touched her chin, and found it dripping with *something*. It took a few moments, but she half-opened her eyes.

Her vision was blurry, but even that couldn't distort the view of her fingers being bright red in places.

I'm, she thought, too weak even to feel horror. *I'm coughing up blood—Great.*

She looked up slowly, just about ready to collapse. She was heavily wounded, her mental endurance was at it's last strand, and she was still surrounded by at least three hundred Oblivions; she knew all this. Her magic came back suddenly with a twinge, but she didn't dare use it; she was on the verge of blacking out already.

It's too much, she thought weakly, almost wanting to die, unconsciously curling up. *There's still so many, and I can't last much longer. I'm so sorry, Keith.*

The moment she thought of Keith's name, her mind reeled. All he'd done for her—cared for her, given her a home and friends, and essentially raised her. With her gone, he'd be devastated. And worse, if the Oblivions were still alive, they could attack the still-sleeping city and kill everyone, including him.

Her fists clenched. *No,* she thought quietly. *Not while I'm still alive.*

So she stood up slowly, holding her warpblade and drawing on her last bits of strength. As she did so, her body began to glow again, but it lasted much longer than the quick changes she'd done before. Breathing heavily, she looked up at the last of the Oblivions, her face determined. "You won't get away with this," she growled in a low voice, the glow becoming it's brightest yet, met with intense hisses.

When it faded, Brianna's clothes were still unchanged, due to her wearing normal clothes. She held two warpblades in her hands—one attack, the other defense—but two more floated beside her, the speed and finisher variants. Every other second, the warpblades glowed faintly along the edges.

The Oblivions only stalled for a moment, then they resumed the attack.

Armed with an unshakable concentration, Brianna didn't notice her pain, and jumped forward. Spinning in mid flight, she slashed at Oblivions on both sides. As she did so, her two floating warpblades spun rapidly with a mind of their own, creating aerial shockwaves that slammed many away. And when she righted herself, she merely jumped off the ground, propelling herself upward.

High in the air, her hands began glowing different colors. The sky directly above her gathered a thick layer of clouds, and the air became charged. Multiple lightning bolts struck downward, splitting apart in mid-air and striking large parts of the ground. In addition, the clouds spit two tornadoes downward, whipping through the Oblivions.

She fell downward where the remaining ones were intending to tear her apart. She didn't give them a chance to; an icy storm erupted right below her, softening her descent and freezing the unfortunate Oblivions solid. Before she landed completely, she pulled eight fire-whips out of nowhere and destroyed them.

Only then did she touch the ground. And no more Oblivions were around her after she did.

Breathing heavily, she looked around her fiercely, ready for more. Then she thought of her friends.

Whether it was instinct or the drive itself, she started floating upward on her own.

High in the air, she saw them some distance away, still fighting hard against their own separated groups. The Oblivions numbers were no longer in the thousands, but they were still a threat: Emmy's and Veren's movements were lethargic, and it was clear they were in terrible pain. So without thinking, her hands both glowed a dark blue. The magic took the form of twin magic balls, flying down at each group.

Halfway there, they burst open and expanded, becoming mini black holes.

All Oblivions from both groups were pulled upward into the air against their will. Emmy and Veren were exempted from this pull, but Brianna was already at work. As the Oblivions fought helplessly against the pull, she twisted, then began spinning in midair. Faster and faster she went, until the air itself began to spin around her, like a tornado, until all the Oblivions were in her grip.

Then, with all her might, she redirected the spin, and sent every Oblivion flying up out of sight.

Her expression weak, she floated downward slowly, aiming toward Emmy and Veren. The Oblivions never came back down when she landed a minute later.

The three of them could barely stand, and their clothes were torn in multiple places. They were bruised and bleeding, and their muscles would be sore for weeks. Emmy and Veren said something, but her ears heard nothing. As she looked, unable to think at all, she unconsciously slipped out of her new drive. Her warpblades followed suit with flashes of light.

The pain split her head open, and she struggled against it, but it was too strong. She blacked out.

DAYS IN THE HOSPITAL

Across her, Veren was barely able to breathe, let alone move. But still he struggled against it, looking down with a hand clutching his chest. "We can't thank you enough, Bri," he said weakly.

"Yeah," Emmy rasped, clutching at her side. "Thank you."

Brianna never answered though, which made him weakly furrow his eyebrows. He flinched; there was a cut directly on his eyebrow muscle, and it hurt to move it. "Bri?" he rasped, but there was still no answer.

With what little strength he had, he looked up.

Brianna fell to the ground, her head lolling to the side. She didn't move.

"Bri?" he rasped out, stumbling toward her. "Bri!"

He collapsed, breathing heavily and willingly going to his knees as he felt a deep fear. "Bri! Bri, wake up!" he shouted hoarsely, shaking her hard, despite the pain it caused in his arms. "You gotta wake up! Bri!"

"Quiet!" Emmy cried out, though she gave a little cry of pain after that. This surprised him long enough for Emmy to lay her head on Bri's chest, her bloodied eyebrows furrowed.

She withdrew her head, her hair a mess. "It's okay," she rasped out between breaths. "She's breathing, and she has a heartbeat—I think she's just unconscious."

Veren literally collapsed on the spot, relieved beyond words.

Just then, the ground almost directly beside them turned black, and began to swirl.

"Oh, what now!" Emmy cried out, at her limit.

A pair of large claws dug out of the ground, then a shape dove straight out of the ground, kicking up a large storm of dust along the way—so thick that Emmy and Veren coughed hard, which hurt them more. It also prevented them from seeing what had come out of the ground.

A low growl soon told them exactly who.

Fenrir moved beside them, looking at all three of them quickly, his fur standing on end.

"Fenrir," Veren rasped, in too much pain to think. "Where were you?"

"What happened?"

Veren cried out, clutching his head, and he vaguely saw Emmy do the same. Fenrir's projected voice had just hit him like a hammer blow, despite being the same volume as always.

"Don't do that!" he yelled out, breathing heavily before his chest started to burn. "Ow."

Fenrir drew back, appeared to think this over, then took one claw and quickly dug it into the ground, drawing a message letter by letter.

"What happened?" Emmy read aloud quietly, looking up at him slowly. "We were attacked."

"There were so many Oblivions!" Veren rasped, groaning as his side hurt. "Where were you?"

Fenrir growled slightly, but he apparently forced himself to ignore it. Then he saw Brianna's form, and his fur stood on end again. He rather jerkily gestured at his message in the ground.

"We—" Emmy tried to say, only to cough hard. "We don't know."

"She's alive though," Veren whispered, now too weak to shout, or really care where Fenrir had been. "She's alive," he said, to himself, one hand on his head.

Fenrir's form eased a little, but then he started flinching a little, particularly around his nose and eyes. Then he did something simple but realistic. He sneezed.

Except for one detail—thick black smoke curled from his nostrils afterward.

Emmy and Veren stared uncomprehendingly at this new and completely-out-of-nowhere development, and they didn't say anything. What the hell had that been about? Fenrir looked just as confused and surprised as they did.

After that, Veren's sense of what happened become very blank, and he knew no more.

June 18, 2028

Veren groaned, his head swimming with a massive headache. Despite that, he struggled to wake up. Recurring pains in his chest, his arms, and his legs made it difficult to focus though.

"What?" he breathed, only to feel a hand easily push him back down. The gentle push had expertly avoided any of his wounded areas.

"Don't get up, Veren," he heard, but he couldn't see the voice's owner yet as his eyes were closed. "You need to rest."

He obeyed, but he still opened his eyes. His vision didn't clear for a few seconds, but it did slowly. When it did, he saw a man standing near him, who looked familiar somehow.

He later recognized him as Noah.

"What—what happened?" he whispered, blinking slowly and groaning a little from his headache. "There were so many of them."

"Bri," he heard to his left.

Blinking faintly, he turned his head toward the source; Emmy was lying on a hospital bed, heavily bandaged underneath the temporary gown.

"What?" he asked slowly, his brain having trouble processing.

She looked at him, her face heavily cut up but not bleeding anymore. "Bri," she repeated, flinching from a pain in her side, where her hand was. "She saved us."

"She—" he breathed, only to somehow stagger where he lay. Emmy's words brought back a rush of feelings and memories, and he staggered upward. "Bri!" he cried out, only to cry out; it felt as though his ribs were broken; so great was the pain.

"You can't get up yet, you're still too weak," Noah said harshly, pushing him back down. "If you start walking around, you'll only make things worse!"

Grunting, he looked up at Noah. "I have to know if Bri's all right!" he cried out desperately. "I'll drag myself there if I have to, but I need to know she's okay!"

"And I'm with Veren," Emmy said determinedly. "We need to see Bri."

Noah sighed as he pinched the bridge of his nose. "And you'll get to," he said, removing his fingers, "but you need medical attention first, then you'll see your friend."

Veren struggled with himself, then slowly sank back into his hospital bed, weary and worried. "Fine," he said finally, resigned. "Just please, heal us fast so we can see her as soon as possible."

June 19, 2028

"This is ridiculous," Veren complained, stifling a groan as a healer worked on his ribs.

Emmy looked over at him, her left arm in the process of being healed. "You want to see Bri because you're worried about her," she whispered softly, her face twitching a bit as she felt a twinge of pain. "I am too, but complaining won't speed up time."

"Well, it's not like I can do much else," he said, sighing as he slumped against the bed. As he did so, the current healer was replaced by another, who continued the healing.

"True, but—" she started to say, stopping as she heard the door open. "Keith!"

"Hey," he said, walking inside quickly. The bags under his eyes still hadn't faded from his abrupt awakening last night.

"How's Bri?" Veren asked instantly, sitting upright, only to stifle a groan and get scolded by the healer.

Keith sighed, running a hand over his face. "They still won't let me see her," he said heavily. "They won't tell me anything, other than they need absolute focus on her."

"What is wrong with them?" he demanded. "Why can't we know what happened to her?"

"Wait," Emmy said quietly, but in a way that everyone heard her. "Keith, what's that on your arm?"

Keith glanced at his right arm, where a faint purple-black tendril clung to his skin, swirling and phasing randomly. "Oh this?" he said without concern, holding up his arm. "This magic is so Fenrir can hear everything we say."

"Why?" Veren said, blinking.

"Fenrir can't fit through the door," he said with a brief mild tone. "But since he's just as worried as we are, he wants to know what's going on."

"Well, he's not gonna wait much longer," Veren said grimly, throwing off his hospital blankets and staggering up slowly.

Keith watched him carefully. "I can't stop you?" he asked gently.

"No," he answered bluntly, already walking out of the room, though with a major limp. Keith watched him go, then glanced at Emmy, who was also staggering out of bed.

"Veren," she said as she got up, her voice a mix of understanding, exasperation, and apology. She looked at Keith after standing up.

Keith tilted his head toward the door briefly. "Go," he said gently, watching her go afterward.

Then after a second's reflection, he turned and followed them.

It didn't take the three of them long to find where Brianna was being cared for, thanks to Keith's directions.

Brianna lay on a simple hospital bed, much like the ones they had lain on minutes ago, though there were small bloodstains. She was alive, as was clearly evident by her steady breathing. Her eyes were closed though, and her expression was peaceful as she lay there, unmoving. Overall, she looked fine, but the doctor's tension said otherwise.

"Tell me the situation here," Keith said, looking around at them.

They looked at them, but no one said anything.

Veren stepped forward, breathing heavily and glancing at Brianna's face repeatedly. "Please," he rasped, his voice weak. "Tell me what's wrong, don't keep us in the dark!"

Noah sighed heavily, then slowly stepped forward, his hands behind his back. "I'm just not sure how to tell you three," he said quietly, his voice subdued. "I know you care a lot about her."

"Please," Emmy begged, forcing her gaze away from Brianna, tears shining in her eyes. "Tell us."

He looked down, silent for awhile. "She—" he started slowly, only to stop. "Due to her multiple uses of magic and drives, she suffered a lot of damage. She went over her limit, and—her brain lapsed into a coma."

Keith staggered backward, hitting the wall as he did so. Veren and Emmy didn't notice this as they were confused.

"Coma?" Veren said slowly, looking at Noah. "What's that?"

Noah drew a hand over his face, sighing heavily. "Basically," he said heavily, removing his hand. "Her heart beats, her lungs breathe, but her mind is shut down—she's just an empty shell. And she may never recover."

"What?" Emmy rasped in horror, her legs suddenly weak.

Veren's legs gave out, and he sank to his knees, barely noticing the spike of pain. "No," he rasped, his vision blurring rapidly. "No—no no no!"

He collapsed against Emmy, holding her tightly around the legs, and just sobbed. The room filled with his cries, and all three of them were in tears.

It was much later in the day, and the doctors had finally given them some privacy, though they were not to leave the hospital wing. Keith had left the room some time ago, and he was still devastated as they all were. Veren was at Brianna's side, his face in the sheets, staining them. Emmy was leaning her head against the wall, her face hidden.

"This can't be happening," Veren rasped into the sheets for the third time, his voice muffled.

Emmy did not respond.

He looked up, his eyes red and his face heavily tear-stained. "Bri," he rasped out, his voice cracking. His hand tightened around hers, which did not respond. "And our last talk was over a stupid argument—man I'm an idiot! If I'd have known this would happen, I wouldn't have gotten angry!"

"Stop it!" Emmy yelled, making him jerk with fear.

Emmy slowly removed herself from the wall, stood facing it for a moment, then turned and walked toward him. Her face was just as red and tear-stained as his was.

"Beating yourself up isn't helping anythingm" she said so quietly and subdued it surprised both of them. She slowly got down on her knees beside him, looking at Brianna.

Veren sighed heavily, looking down and terribly close to trembling. "I know," he whispered quietly. "But—I feel so helpless. The doctors can't do anything, so what chance would I have?"

Emmy placed a hand on his shoulder, her eyes weak. "I know this is hard for you," she said. "It's hard for all of us."

"But it's worse for me," he whispered weakly, starting to sob again. "Not only have I lost a dear friend—I lost a truly great woman who loved me dearly, and whom I loved dearly back"

"Veren, she's not lost!" she said, with far more exasperation than she intended to show. She drew back after Veren flinched a bit, taking in a breath, a hand in her hair. *My nerves are frayed,* she thought faintly.

Shaking her head a little, she looked back at him. "She's just sleeping," she said, as gently as she could.

"But she may not wake up again," he whispered weakly, fresh tears falling and staining the sheets below.

"She may also wake up someday," she whispered, her hand gripping his shoulder. "And on that day, I want us both to be there for her."

Veren made a small noise, simply breathing for awhile. But just as he was about to say something, the door opened and a young man entered.

"Um, excuse me," he said, looking at them with coal-black eyes. "Are you three Brianna, Emmy, and Veren?"

Veren blinked, but Emmy narrowed her eyes faintly, looking at him. Something was familiar about him—his eyes, his black hair.

"Uh, yes," Veren said, slowly standing, wiping at his eyes. "I'm Veren, this is Emmy, and—" he said, stopping at the end.

The young man glanced at Bri, then he shifted a bit. "Is this a bad time?" he asked hesitantly.

"Well," Veren said, then sighed as he looked down. "Yeah"

"Wait a minute," Emmy said, standing up. "Who are you?"

"I'm James" he said simply, looking directly at her.

Emmy instantly tensed while Veren glanced at her. He knew what this meant, but his expression also said he was feeling guilty. After all, they'd completely forgotten about him since they'd brought him back.

"And what are you doing here?" she asked bluntly, her eyes suspicious.

James blinked at her sudden hostility, looking at her. "Um, I was told you three were part of my past—the one I can't remember," he said, looking from one to the other. "I'm hoping you could help me with that."

"As if," she huffed, crossing her arms.

"Uh, please excuse us," Veren said quickly, pulling her out of the room by the arm, leaving James to stand there staring after him, confused.

"What are you doing?" he demanded quickly, once they were out of earshot. "You can't just treat him like that because of what he did!"

"So I slipped a little," she said quietly, looking away. "When I look at his face, I'm reminded of what he tried to do, and the guilt I feel for how hard it was on you two."

"I get that part," he said, moving himself into her field of vision. "But James is not Setxis. That personality is gone, for good."

"Don't you think I know that?" she yelled, making him jolt. After her outburst though, she shrank back a little. "But I can't bring myself to act friendly to him, not when I'm reminded of what he nearly did."

Veren sighed, a hand over his face for a few seconds. "Look, Emmy," he said, "I understand your issues with him, and while I can't relate to them, I have my own issues with Setxis."

She looked up at him slowly, waiting.

"Even though I didn't know Bri at the time, Setxis and his guards were after Brianna from the moment she met them," he continued. "And they continued to chase her long after she found us. That's about eight years' worth of chasing my friend, and my girlfriend. I hated him for that stupid pursuit, and I still do. But I know James is not the one who did those things. And I will act friendly toward James, knowing he is not to blame."

Emmy was silent for awhile, glancing down in thought. "Sound logic, Veren," she said finally, her tone faint with admiration. "I never thought about it like that—and I envy you being able to do that"

Veren put his hand on her shoulder, managing a small smile, though it took a lot of effort. "Thank you," he said softly. "All I'm asking is for you to try acting friendly to James. That's it, just try. And I'll do my best to help should you slip up."

She closed her eyes, breathing in and out faintly. "Okay," she said, opening her eyes again with a small smile. "I'll try, Veren."

He nodded, removing his hand, then he tilted his head toward the hospital room. "Now, let's go back and talk to James, okay?" he said simply.

She nodded after a moment, and slowly walked back with him to the room. As soon as they entered, James looked up from Brianna, his expression still hesitant.

"Is there a problem between us?" he asked, concerned.

"There was," Emmy said, glancing away for a moment, her face still red from crying. "But it'll take too long to explain if we don't start from the beginning."

"Sit down, James," Veren said, doing so himself. "This story will be quite a shock."

"No!" James exclaimed, upright and gripping his head. "It can't be!"

The exclamation was his latest outburst, specifically from the raw shock he was feeling. Veren and Emmy were still seated, their expressions mixed.

"Trust us, Set—" Emmy started, only to break off. "Trust us, James. We all vividly remember what you did."

"I still can't believe it!" he yelled, groaning as he slammed his fists against the wall. "I've been manipulated and forced to do those terrible things. I should be in prison!"

"But you aren't the one who did those acts," Veren said, his voice hard. "Someone planted that personality into you, against your will. We need to know who."

James sighed heavily, turning slowly. "That's the problem though—I don't remember" he said quietly. "When I reach for my missing memories, all I get is this blank nothing."

Veren pinched the bridge of his nose, struggling against his frustration. *Calm down*, he forcibly told himself, taking deep breaths. *You'll find this person in due time.*

"Well," Emmy said faintly, "we do know this person is a woman, but that's it."

James glanced at her, but his expression was tortured, his breathing heavy. He glanced back and forth between them, then looked over at Brianna, who was still resting peacefully. With a weak noise, he rushed over, falling to his knees beside her.

Veren instinctively made a move forward, but he managed to stop himself.

Gripping her one visible hand in both of his, he lowered his head. "Bri," he rasped out. "I don't know if you can hear this, but this is James. The things I've done to you, and your friends, they weren't done by me. You probably already know this, but I'm so, so sorry, Bri! What else can I say?"

Veren's hand curled into a fist briefly, his mind working on the sight of James holding her hand. He took in a deep breath, then let it out, slowly walking toward him. Emmy stood up slowly, having watched this. It took James several seconds to notice Veren beside him.

"Thank you for what you've said," he said simply, slowly pulling James into a standing position. "You've said it all."

James nodded slowly, glancing at Bri, but he didn't say anything.

"But for future reference," Veren said faintly, rubbing his head, "Bri is my girlfriend."

James looked between Bri and him in shock, and had already opened his mouth, presumably to apologize.

But Veren held up a hand, shaking his head a little. "It's okay," he said, the words coming less easily than he would have liked. "Just don't make a habit of that, okay?"

Taking in a shaky breath, James nodded fast. "Agreed," he said.

JUMP-START

It was fairly late in the day, and many of the students were starting to wrap up their training routines outside. And with the sudden-yet-mild heat wave, they were glad for it.

Veren and Emmy were alone in the hospital wing, inside Bri's room. Veren sat on a chair beside her bed, his face downcast. Emmy stood against the wall on the other side, her gaze distant. The room was silent except for the sounds of their breathing.

Veren sat there, his mind numb as he faintly played with Bri's fingers. They moved when pushed, but they did nothing on their own.

He gripped her hand with both of his, staring at her face for a long while, brushing a small strand of hair out of her face. She looked so peaceful, so relaxed. It was as if she'd never wake up.

His hands began to shake, and he closed his eyes, but it failed to stop the tears. His whole body shook as well, and he pressed her hand against his forehead, wishing there were something—anything!—that he could do.

He didn't hear or notice the faint footsteps, then a hand slipped over his.

His breath staggered a little, then he slowly raised his head, looking up. Emmy stood there beside him, her hand staying on top of his. She looked back at him for a few moments, then gave him a small sad smile. Her expression said it all.

Breathing faintly, he slowly and sadly smiled back, showing he understood. He looked back at Bri as Emmy withdrew her hand. He slowly wiped at his eyes, then stood up with a sigh. It was the first sound he'd made in hours, and his muscles were cramped.

"A month and a half," he said faintly, his voice weak from little use, "and no change—I don't know if I can continue like this anymore. Every single day? It's too much."

"We have to," she said with finality, glancing at him. "As much as you may want to, your idea to jump-start her brain is risky. It could make things worse."

"Or it could revive her," he said, trailing off.

Who was he kidding anyway? As much as he wanted Bri back, he didn't want her back at the cost his idea could have.

Specifically, he'd discussed this with the doctors at length—to try to jump-start her brain with electricity, as the brain was essentially a mass of electrical impulses, or so they had said. It didn't make much sense to him. They said it was an intriguing idea, but they were reluctant to try it, fearing the risks. They knew using electricity to jump-start her brain could just as easily kill her as revive her. And he had initially wanted to try it anyway, despite the risks.

And that disturbed him: that he'd been willing to try something like that, even for a moment, just to get Bri back. *Damn darkness!* he cursed in his thoughts before he slumped.

Why was he pretending otherwise? The darkness only enhanced what was already there.

Emmy saw the emotions flit across his face, and she sympathized, slowly putting a hand on his shoulder. He felt it, but he gave no sign.

Eventually, footsteps sounded, drawing Emmy's attention. In her surprise, her hand slipped off his shoulder, though he took longer to notice either of these developments.

"Keith!" Emmy greeted.

He didn't acknowledge her greeting, or even appear to notice their prescene, which made her blink several times. His appearance was haggard, though it was very subtle. And the sadness he was visibly radiating made him look older than he was.

"No change," he rasped faintly, more to himself than anyone else.

Veren finally looked over, just in time to see Keith approach Bri, getting down on his knees beside her. Veren hastily stood up. And after a few moments, Keith's hand slowly pushed a strand of hair out of her face. His touch was gentle, almost a loving caress. It was a lot like Veren had done some time ago.

The two teens looked at each other slowly, then back at Keith. "Um, Keith?" Emmy said gently, slowly approaching him.

He didn't respond.

"Keith," Veren said, a bit firmer.

"What?" he said, his tone almost offhand. He hadn't even looked at them.

They glanced at each other, really worried now. Something was definitely up.

"Keith, we know you're a caring man," Emmy said, glancing at Bri. "And we love that about you. But—" she said, trailing off at the end.

"Why the special interest in Bri?" said Veren, more bluntly than he'd intended, sighing a bit. "The doctors said you've visited every day, and most of the time you've been a wreck. Why?"

Keith closed his eyes, but he didn't reply. Instead, he stood up slowly, sighing heavily. Then he turned and walked outside the room, motioning for them to follow.

Glancing at each other again, they quickly walked after him.

"You deserve to know" he said when he finally stopped, as though each word was difficult to utter.

"Well don't just stand there," Emmy said, looking at him. "Spit it out"

He glanced at her, then looked into space. "Do you two know how I found Brianna years ago?" he said faintly.

They looked at each other and found that no, they didn't. "No," Veren said, looking back at the sleeping Brianna. "Nothing other than you found her."

He nodded faintly, still staring off into space. "Right," he said, as if speaking to the air. "Well, you both know Bri lived in this city for six years, dealing with those guards," he continued, the last word having an edge.

"One day, she was attacked by Oblivions. I don't know how they found her, but they did. She was trapped, and my first instinct was to protect her, but I didn't know who she was. And later, we talked a bit, and she told me her name."

"That moment changed my view of things forever," he finished faintly, looking down.

"But why?" Emmy asked simply, her expression worried. "How did her name change things?"

He didn't answer that. Instead, he continued. "I wanted to say so many things, but luckily, I thought considerably before I said anything," he whispered. "So I acted like nothing had changed—I still wonder if that was the best thing I could've done."

"Keith!" Veren breathed firmly, his voice a little strained. "Tell us how her name changed things."

He slowly turned, looking straight at Veren, his eyes full of many different emotions. "Because, Veren," he said heavily, "Brianna is my daughter."

"Well—" Veren started to say, but stopped, the meaning sinking in hard. "Huh?"

"You—" Emmy said after several seconds, sounding dazed. "But she—how did—what!"

Despite himself, Veren glanced at her briefly; he'd never seen Emmy speechless before.

Keith looked at them for several long moments, then he sighed and moved past them, heading back towards Bri's bed. It took them a few seconds before they could bring themselves to follow, staring at each other and at Keith.

Keith stood beside the sleeping Bri, his expression heart-wrenching. Fresh tears only worsened his appearance.

He slowly extended a hand, brushing against her forehead and hair, lingering there for awhile. Then he bent down, kissed her forehead, then withdrew.

She never stirred the whole time.

He audibly choked back a sob, then he turned and walked out slowly. He made no attempt to hide or wipe away his tears—as if he didn't care if others saw them.

And long after he was gone, Emmy and Veren were still in shock about what he'd said.

Much later that day, Emmy and Veren had reluctantly left the hospital wing, knowing from experience how far to test the doctor's patience. And while they didn't talk with Keith again, they went to talk with Fenrir, who had come every day that he could. Meanwhile, a male nurse tended to Bri, as best as could be done. Eventually, he left for the night, but there was a period before the night shift took over.

The sun was more than half-hidden by the horizon, and the light was fading quickly. Brianna continued to slumber peacefully, unaware of anything around her.

Before the light faded completely though, a swirling black vortex appeared silently on the floor beside the window.

It hovered there for a few moments. It was too small to belong to a Fenrir. Then a column of darkness sprang upward, eventually taking a human shape. The darkness cloaked the figure as it swirled around, fading away after a moment. The figure opened her blue eyes, quickly adapting to the fading light.

She was a tall woman, standing inches above Bri. Brianna herself was fairly tall, but she was an inch shorter than Keith. The woman brushed her long brown-black hair out of her face and looked straight at the sleeping Bri with a strange expression. She remained silent throughout her stare.

She wore a dark-purple shirt with a simple black belt, which had a blue diamond set in the buckle, wrapped around her midriff to keep it firm. She also wore a pair of red-violet pants, which had been fashioned to have the appearance of jeans, reaching to just below her knees. The rest of her legs were covered by brown stockings, except for a small bit of skin between her pants and stockings. Over these, she wore a pair of sneakers, which were mainly white with hints of dark green.

She stayed silent for awhile, then she stepped closer to Bri as the sun was disappearing beneath the horizon.

"It's such a shame this happened to you," she said finally, sitting down beside her. Her voice was thoughtful, with a number of emotions underlying it; if Brianna had been awake, she would have recognized her voice.

"You've done very well, Bri," she continued, tilting her head with a small smile. "You and your friends did very well against that army. They wouldn't have killed you—I made sure of that—but I had to make sure you were progressing. And you surpassed my expectations."

She sighed, brushing a hand through her hair. "But I made a mistake," she stated, even though Bri did not react at all. "I had no idea of your limits, or even what would have happened if you hadn't slipped into this coma. A dreadful slip-up on my part, one I regret immensely."

She was silent, looking off into the distance for awhile, then back at Bri. "Your hair looks a lot like Keith's in color, as befits his daughter," she said to nobody, smiling a bit, her hand touching a few strands. "But you don't have his eyes."

Moments afterward, she stood up, glancing at the empty doorway. "Must remember to thank Veren for his idea," she said, chuckling slightly to herself and holding up her hands.

Her hands started glowing yellow, and electricity arced between her fingers, almost faster than eyes could follow. "Ugh, gotta lower the current," she said to herself. "I don't want to kill her."

Through her conscious effort, the electricity racing between her fingers slowed down, finally moving with such slowness that it was surreal. It was just for show though, and it did not reflect the changes she was making. When she was confident, she slowly looked at Brianna. "Ready," she said to herself.

Then she carefully touched her fingers to parts of Bri's head, mildly messing up her hair. Seconds later, electricity surged through Bri, her entire body twitching, though there was a lack of this where the vital organs were situated. After a split second, she withdrew her fingers an inch, watching carefully for any signs of stirring.

When none happened after a few seconds, she slowly and carefully repeated the process.

Minutes passed as she repeated the process. The light outside was fading rapidly, but Brianna showed no sign of activity beyond the induced twitching. And with her careful touch, nothing was damaged with the brief jolts.

On the tenth minute, the woman withdrew for a small break, lightly flexing her fingers about five times. When she returned to try again though, she saw it: Brianna's foot twitched, and it wasn't her doing.

She waited, completely still, watching Bri carefully in case it was just a coincidence.

It was not; Bri's fingers curled slightly, having previously been in a relaxed position.

The woman smiled, rather tenderly, as she looked on. Brianna's consciousness was returning *very* slowly but surely. "My work here is done," she said simply, patting the girl's forehead twice before stepping back. "I'll look forward to your return, in time."

And with that, darkness slowly wrapped around her, and when it faded away, she was gone.

Darkness surrounded her, a medley of confusing sensations that made no sense.

She stirred, every part of her sluggish to respond. She knew not where she was, what she was doing, or even her own name. And because she was so sluggish, time passed slowly as she tried to make sense of things. Eventually, she opened her eyes.

At first, all she saw was a blur of color. But as she stared with confused eyes, they began to change; they darkened and gained a form. Her brain was eventually able to see the world clearly, and she saw the room she was lying in. She could not make out where it was though.

Without realizing it, she raised her head a bit, her eyes wandering over herself. She looked at her hand and at her twitching fingers, trying to figure out why they were doing so. But what was she lying on, and what was she covered with? The slowness of her recovery evoked a strange feeling in her, but she could only tell that it was a negative feeling.

Still looking at her hand, she tried to make it move, to stop her fingers twitching. Her first few attempts, labored and strained, did nothing. Then she succeeded. Her fingers slowed then stopped. She tried again, and her fingers moved as commanded. She was recovering, albeit still very slowly.

Turning her head slowly, she then tried to move her hand. It jerked several times, but it did as she commanded, slowly moving toward the thing covering her. It took her awhile before she could grasp it, and then even longer before she pulled the cover off her. Sitting up took much more effort, but her strength was slowly returning.

She stared at her legs, trying to figure out why she was here in the first place, and where *here* was. All it got her was an ache in her head, so she shook her head, and tried the same process on her legs. They took longer, but her command of her body was coming along well. The effort to move her legs swung them over the side of the thing she lay on.

Sitting like that, she took a minute to look around, blinking slowly. Maybe— she could move around, and try to find out where she was?

Looking down, she moved herself in short bursts closer to the edge. Her legs went dangling at first, then her feet touched the hard ground. She tested it a bit, to make sure it was hard enough, all the while feeling odd. Was she even strong enough to move in this manner?

She felt there was only one way to find out. Her hands still gripping the bed tightly, she slowly slid herself off.

Her legs wobbled, then she collapsed onto her knees. Only her grip on the bed kept her from falling to the floor.

She cried out, her body spiking with a dull ache, her body curling automatically. Though she didn't notice it, her cry had been hoarse. But without knowing it, she fought against the ache, struggling to stand up with her recovering strength. She eventually succeeded, again without knowing she had done so.

Using the bed to support herself, she looked around, her eyes falling upon an opening in the room. Maybe that way could tell her where she was.

She struggled forward, using everything within reach to support herself, as her legs were still wobbling. One person she didn't know at all was badly startled by her appearance, but she paid little attention to him.

As she limped throughout the area, she began to get flashes in her mind, mostly of faces; one of an adult male with amber eyes, his appearance giving her a feeling of warmth and safety; another male showed up, younger with blue eyes, who made her entire body feel warm, best as she could tell; and the third was female, with blond hair and green eyes, who gave her a different warm feeling.

Some of those faces weren't normal though. One was of a large creature, with sharp claws, teeth, and yellow eyes. Looking at him gave her warmth though, the same way as with the female face. And the last one was of an all-black creature, also with yellow eyes, who made her feel completely cold inside.

But other than the feelings, she couldn't make sense of them.

She eventually stumbled upon yet another opening, which she went through without thinking. Some distance away though, she saw other people standing around, one much larger than the other.

It took her several moments before she recognized them as the faces she'd thought of earlier.

Slightly earlier, the sun had disappeared under the horizon, and Veren stood just outside the school with Emmy and Fenrir.

No change? Fenrir asked, speaking to Veren, and arranging it so Emmy could hear as well. He had just arrived not moments ago.

Veren shook his head, sighing with sad eyes. "None," he said simply, glancing at Emmy before he looked up. "But we'll keep waiting. She may not wake up, but she might wake up anyway."

I don't like this, he said, growling to himself. *Bri sleeping in this manner you call a coma. It leaves this pit in my stomach. I have never experienced this before.*

"None of us like it, Fenrir." Emmy said, a hand briefly on his fur. "We all feel that same pit in our stomachs, and we hate it. But we will wait nonetheless."

Fenrir growled again, low in tone, then his eyes narrowed in thought. Then he looked from Emmy to Veren. *I have been puzzled lately,* he said in their minds. *You remember the night Bri fell asleep?*

"How could we forget?" Veren said, and it came out harsher than he meant. As soon as he said it, he immediately recoiled, regretting it. "Yeah, we remember."

Fenrir took no offense and only glanced at him. *So you remember when I breathed smoke?*

Emmy nodded, but her brow was furrowed. "Yeah," she said slowly. "But how could that have happened? I've never heard of Fenrir's being able to do that. And aren't streams of smoke usually followed by fire?"

Nor have I witnessed this among my kind, or among the other animals, except those who use it naturally, Fenrir said, growling to himself. *It is strange that I can suddenly breathe smoke, possibly with fire not too far behind, but I have not been able to repeat the experience. I sometimes feel burning in my nostrils though, among other sensations.*

Veren held a hand on his chin, thinking. "Maybe," he said slowly, almost thoughtfully, "maybe it's one of those rare things, like those diseases that not many get"

So you're saying that I'm diseased, Veren? Fenrir said, an unmistakable edge in his growl.

He looked up, and almost gulped when he saw Fenrir an inch away from his face. The strain showed on his face, but he kept his voice even. "No, Fenrir," he said carefully. "I'm saying that you might have something unique and rare, something very few other living beings may have."

Fenrir was silent for a moment, then he snorted, and Veren nearly gagged from the blast of hot air in his face. *Flattery becomes you, Veren,* he said. *Your words are just as twisted as a snake.*

Veren wasn't sure what to say, so he just said, "Thank you," but slower than normal.

Fenrir's head backed off, though he was still looking at Veren. *"And that, among other things, is why you're worthy of being Bri's mate."*

Veren turned bright red. He wanted so much to say he was only in a relationship with Bri, not married to her—which was similar to what mate meant for wolves—yet, he couldn't bring himself to, partly because Fenrir might not understand, as mating meant anything from a relationship to children for his kind. And also because the thought of being married to Bri didn't sound so bad.

Sure he'd only turned fifteen a few months ago, but there was always the future to consider.

"So when's the wedding, lover boy?" Emmy whispered in his ear, startling him badly.

"I-I don't know what you're talking about!" he said very quickly, still red, until seconds later a thought occurred to him. "Wait, why didn't you say anything earlier?"

Emmy smiled a bit, giggling slightly. "I didn't want to interrupt, though there were several things I could have said."

He raised a faint eyebrow. "What happened to the always-speak-my-mind Emmy?" he asked, surprised.

"Don't get me wrong, I'll still speak my mind," she said seriously, a friendly arm around his shoulder. "I'm just learning that sometimes it's better to keep my mouth shut. At least until the right time, anyway."

We're all growing, Veren thought wryly, even as he smiled. Bri was slowly learning the social aspect of the world and about herself, and Emmy was learning that speaking her mind had it's place.

But what was he learning? The closest thing he could think of was leadership. *Hmm—*

During this little exchange, Fenrir glanced away. And he sniffed at the air audibly. They eventually noticed. Emmy removed her arm from Veren's shoulder.

"What?" Veren asked, looking up at him, blinking.

Fenrir did not answer, but continued to sniff at the air. Then he tensed. *I smell Bri.*

Both of them blinked, then Emmy tilted her head. "You mean you smell her from here?"

No, I don't mean her sleeping body, he said, sniffing again, still tense. *There is a difference in a person's scent when they are awake and when they are asleep, and I'm not smelling the latter. But how can this be?*

He turned toward the school, still sniffing. *I can only assume that Bri is*—he started to say, but then he stopped, staring straight at the school.

Emmy and Veren tried to see what was wrong, but failing to do that, they looked at the school too. And when they did, they stopped, their faces paling.

Brianna stood at the entrance, wearing only her hospital gown, and leaning against the wall for support. She looked completely lost.

"Bri," the three of them breathed at the same time, though Fenrir's only came out as a small growl. Then it all happened so fast—the three of them practically jumped on Bri, hugging her half to death, and in Veren's case, almost smothering her in kisses.

Brianna didn't know how to react though, and only looked around in confusion.

CONVALESCENCE

August 9, 2028

Veren stood in the doorway of Brianna's room, smiling as he watched Emmy talking to Bri, who still lay on her bed. As he watched, Emmy hugged Bri for the fifth time that day. Bri was surprised, yet both bemused and slightly irritated. Also in the room was James, who had recently apologized for his actions for the fifteenth time (not exaggerated in the slightest).

It's been one hectic week, Veren thought grimly, but happy all the same that it resolved the way it did. *James must really feel for what he did to be that open.*

After Brianna had appeared in front of them—scaring them half to death—they'd been overjoyed to have her back, smothering her in hugs and kisses. It wasn't until later that they'd realized Brianna hadn't fully recovered; her body may have awoken, but her brain was still going at its own, much slower pace. She hadn't seemed to recognize them that day, except for their faces. This had caused them great distress and worry, to put it mildly.

So for the past eight days, Bri had been stuck in the hospital to recover, under the watchful eye of the hospital staff. Her progress had been slow but much faster than anyone anticipated or expected. She'd fully recognized Emmy and Keith on the third day, while it took her another two days to remember the romantic times she'd shared with Veren. She remembered their friendship on the third day of course, but it had been difficult to restrain his love for her in those two days' time.

And now, she was almost fully recovered, except for a few small memories here and there that she'd forgotten. The doctors weren't sure those would be recovered, but they were keeping watch regardless.

He couldn't stop staring at her though or hugging or kissing her when they were together. He'd almost lost her, twice, and he was still in disbelief. Happy and relieved but still more-or-less in shock, But more than that, he felt a burning desire to just hug her and never let her go.

"Veren," he heard, startling him. With a small effort, he turned, seeing Keith walking toward him.

"Keith," he greeted, turning to face him, again with a small effort.

Keith did not enter the room though, other than to look inside. "Thank God for small miracles," he said, his voice faint.

"Yeah," Veren agreed wholeheartedly, looking at Bri again. "She's almost completely recovered, except for a few small bits."

"But you haven't told her about me yet," he said, looking straight at him. It wasn't a question.

He hesitated, then sighed, for it was true. "I'm sorry, Keith," he said, worried that he'd be mad. "But I thought telling her ourselves would be the wrong thing to do. This is a matter between you two, and waiting till she was fully recovered seemed best."

Keith looked at him for a moment more, then glanced at the floor, chuckling faintly. "That was my reasoning as well," he said finally. "But it was hard not to say anything."

Veren sighed in relief, nodding. "It has been," he agreed, glancing again at Bri.

They stood in comfortable silence for a moment, then Keith lifted his head. "By the way, there's something you need to know," he said, with some effort. When he had Veren's attention, he continued, "Now that Bri's awake, Skye and Jeena are asking for her, and they want you, Emmy, and James to be there as well."

Veren blinked several times, staring at him in surprise. "Seriously?" he asked. "They want all of us there?"

Keith smiled slightly, nodding. "Yes, they do," he said simply. "As soon as possible."

Veren quickly went inside, telling Emmy, Bri and James about this. Keith watched the whole while as he waited, a tender expression on his face.

About thirty minutes later, Brianna was dressed and ready to go, so the five of them set out.

Brianna, for her part, was glad to finally be out of bed and walking about, even if she still wasn't as strong as she'd have liked. She could see the strain her condition had caused her friends, as it still showed in their faces. The only one who was missing this strain was James, but he didn't know her that well, other than he certainly seemed sincere about regretting what he'd unwittingly done. She still wasn't entirely sure what she felt about him though, considering the circumstances.

Keith seemed tense and withdrawn, though to a small degree, and that worried her. She didn't know why he seemed that way, but she intended to find out later. Emmy was subdued; her gaze was directed downward, and she seemed to struggle not to glance at her. This also worried her, but she was also confused, not knowing why she'd act like that.

And Veren—well, he clung to her, not willing to let her go even for a moment. She liked it when they were close, but this was getting ridiculous.

"So, um,—" she said, breaking the silence. "What happened while I was—asleep?"

"We visited you every daym" Veren answered a bit sadly, his arm wrapped around hers. "James came to see us, we talked quite a lot about things, and uh the three of us slowly became friends,"

"I hope that's okay with you, Brim" James added quickly. "I mean, Emmy and Veren were your friends first,"

"No, it's okaym" she said a bit weakly, discreetly trying to untie Veren's arm from hers for the fifth time. He didn't appear to notice her attempt, but just as she disengaged his arm, he seemed to unconsciously grip her back.

She started feeling a bit frustrated, but she struggled not to say anything. Veren's sudden clinging made perfect sense; he'd almost lost her twice, and had no desire to let her go a third time, no matter what may happen. And she remembered Emmy's words—that she'd learn everything about Veren the closer they got.

But she still secretly hoped he'd lose this grip soon, because she wasn't liking it. And conflicting it all, she wondered if she would say anything, should he not lose this phase.

This and more spanned her thoughts, but their conversation continued uninterrupted. "Seriously, James," she said, looking at him on Veren's left. "I'm okay with it. I'm just feeling disoriented that I've missed a lot of time, including your growing friendship."

He nodded, but then he looked away, his expression troubled. "I still feel terrible about what I've done," he rasped a little. "Mind-control or not."

"It still wasn't your doing, James," Veren said, looking at him. "We've been over this."

Their conversation continued for awhile, James's responses being heavy in subtle tones. Brianna noticed Veren's grip starting to loosen. Breathing a mental sigh of relief, she slowly but carefully worked her way out of his grip, and he didn't notice. So she quickly went to stand by Emmy, also wanting to talk.

"You've been quiet," she said in an undertone, still walking, though stumbling a bit. "What's up?"

"Well, Veren was all over you," Emmy said faintly, looking up at her. "Honestly, I've been wanting to follow his example, just with hugs instead of his more intimate gestures. But I figured you wouldn't like that, so I kept my distance."

"Thank you," she whispered in relief, meaning it. "And you're right, I'm not liking his sudden clinging, even though I know it's perfectly reasonable. Is that wrong?"

Emmy giggled a little, which lifted her worry somewhat. "It definitely seems wrong, but it's actually fairly normal," she said, smiling for a moment. "Don't feel guilty for not liking it. You're allowed to have your own opinion."

She nodded, but just then, she became aware that Veren had noticed she wasn't in his grip anymore. He quickly came over, but when he approached to put them back to an arm-in-arm position, she hesitated backward a step, unwilling. He stopped and opened his mouth to say something.

"We're here," Keith said in front of them, getting their attention.

Veren glanced at Keith, but otherwise still looked at her, his expression questioning. She slowly intertwined her fingers with his, and put on a small smile, hoping her eyes and expression would say it all.

She wasn't entirely sure he got it, but he slowly softened, smiling a bit as he squeezed her hand back. She still got the feeling that they would talk later, knowing Veren, who always liked to know what was wrong, and go on from there.

For the second time, Brianna, Emmy and Veren entered the throne room.

The room was the same as they remembered it—with one major exception. In addition to the human guards, Oathkeepers prowled around the room, and they weren't limited to the ground. And at second glance, the queen's phoenix was nowhere to be seen. This made Bri a little sad; that little guy (or girl?) was a beautiful bird.

Brianna and James gave the Oathkeepers a curious look; the others seemed used to this development by now. Then they simply walked straight toward the two thrones and the figures that sat upon them. This was James's first time though, and he stared around him with awe and interest, trying to take it all in at once. When he noticed an Oathkeeper standing behind him, he quickly turned away, which made him realize that he was falling behind, so he quickly caught up.

At the front, Keith stopped and got down on one knee, bowing his head. The others did the same, though it took a moment for Bri to do so, as she was still a bit weak.

"Please stand," said Skye, standing up himself, approaching them. "You know how much I dislike formalities."

"You're still annoyed," Keith said, with a small smile.

Skye gave him a touche smile. "Always messing with me first, Keith," he said, arms crossed. "Classic."

Jeena gave him *that* cough, and he nodded, turning serious. "Right," he said. "You're all here for the update on the situation. But first, we must bring Brianna up to speed."

Skye looked straight at her, and his expression hinted at sympathy for what she'd endured. "After your incredible fight with that massive army of Oblivions, we knew that Liark could be next. And with Emmy's statement that the army came straight down from the Hearts Mountains, specifically the middle one, we've been focusing our intelligence around there."

He continued a bit grimly: "We've been trying to find out who or what is behind all this. And frankly, we haven't succeeded yet".

"And the Oathkeepers?" Bri asked, glancing up at the nearest one that clung to a support pillar to their left, keeping an eye on them.

He smiled faintly, gesturing at them all. "We've determined that they can best service us this way," he said. "Unlike most magic, they do not need a constant stream of mental endurance to maintain, only for the initial creation. And since their inception, their numbers have been growing, and now we have a large number in service for the city."

He looked back at her, and his smile became wider for a moment. "This includes the task of keeping watch," he said. "So now, Keith's students are no longer required for the job, if that's all okay with you."

Brianna's reaction was one of surprise and relief. As necessary and important as that task had been, she and her friends weren't suited for that job, or it's long periods of boredom. Emmy and Veren didn't react beyond a small smile; presumably, they'd heard this before today. James kept a stoic face though, as this news didn't affect him one way or the other.

"So," Brianna said after a moment. "what's the update, Your Majesty?"

Skye briefly grimaced, and Brianna mentally sweat-dropped: *Oops*, she thought, remembering too late he didn't like that.

But the moment passed. "The update is that due to our failure to locate who or what is responsible for all this, they must be aware of our search, and are concealing themselves."

"I surmised as much," Keith said, glancing away in thought for a moment. "But I fear that one army won't be the last."

Jeena nodded, and spoke, drawing their attentions. "Exactly what we fear as well, Keith," she said, with concern in her tone. "But it did not escape our attention that they targeted Brianna, Emmy, and Veren first, when they could have easily ignored them and attacked this city—they may come after them again".

Bri felt her heart sink, not only at the thought of it actually happening, but also at the feeling that she was right.

Skye nodded, then turned back to them. "And to that end, we would like you three to get your skills back up," he said, grim. "Your work at guard watch has dulled your abilities, as you yourselves have described. For now, we'd like you to build them back up so that when you're ready, we can proceed to the next step."

"If you'd enlighten me, Skye," Keith said, stepping forward. "What is this next step?"

"The next step," Skye said heavily, "is these three will visit the Hearts Mountains personally, search for the one responsible, and confront them if necessary."

"Whoa. Us?" Emmy spoke up, drawing Bri's attention to her surprised face. "It's flattering you think we're that good, but what makes us so important?"

"Because as I mentioned before, the Oblivions targeted you over this city," Jeena said, then her voice became steely. "Whoever is responsible wouldn't go to that trouble without a reason, and we must know all the facts if we are to effectively control this situation. Without it, lives are in danger, and not just human ones."

"Wow, guess you three are important to the villain's plot" James said, with a friendly snarky tone. "Good luck."

"Hey, watch it James," Emmy shot back.

She would've said more, but Veren lightly put some space between them. "We're in an audience," he said lightly, looking from James to Emmy. "Now's not the time."

When he noticed Bri's puzzled look, he quickly leaned in. "That little back-and-forth between them is fairly common," he breathed in an undertone, leaving her to feel odd that her best friend could trade snarks with James, and that he was apparently a snarky type under a stoic face.

And for the second time, Bri was asked to stay a bit longer by Jeena, the only difference being that Skye was sticking around this time. The others went back to Keith's school in the meantime, after they'd reluctantly left her alone, Veren especially.

"When I heard that you'd fallen into a coma, I was devastated," Jeena said, brushing a little hair out of the corner of her eye. "Not just for you, but what it meant for Keith and your friends."

"And imagine our joy and relief when you woke up," Skye said, his left hand holding Jeena's right. A ring glittered there, as did the one on Jeena's left.

"Thank you," she said, humbled that they were worried about her. She fidgeted slightly as she asked, "Hey, is it okay if I ask you two things?"

Jeena smiled warmly, "Of course you can, Bri. Anytime."

She took in a small breath, then stood up straight. "What is the situation with James, considering what he did?" she asked, thinking that he might be killed and it hadn't happened yet. "And also, where's the phoenix you usually have with you, uh, Jeena?"

Skye sighed a bit, his right hand brushing against his blonde bangs. "To answer about James, that is still undetermined," he said gravely. "What he and the other guards did was terrible, but we can't ignore all the evidence that it was not consciously done by his will. We and our advisers discussed this at length, but no one could agree on what should be done, only that something should be done."

He shared a look with Jeena for a moment, then glanced back at Bri. "For now, James is considered to be on parole," he said carefully. "It means we won't do anything yet, but his own actions will decide his fate."

"And we think that, with friends like you, he'll show promise," Jeena added, though with a slight edge. "We're entrusting you all with him."

Bri didn't answer. She felt relieved that James had a chance, but this whole situation made her feel uneasy. She looked up after a few moments. "And the phoenix?" she asked.

Jeena glanced at the empty spot on her throne, then hummed. "Just yesterday, she reached an extremely old age and burst into flames," she said, as if that were normal. "Right now, she's very young, growing slowly on a bed of flaming coals. When she's old enough, she'll return to this spot, should she choose to."

Bri smiled, almost without knowing it. "Cool."

"And now," Skye said, looking at Jeena, "the real reason we asked you to hang back."

"You still don't know who Keith really is, do you," Jeena said. It wasn't a question.

Bri almost answered, but she realized that no, she really didn't. Or at least, she didn't know why she *should* know who he is, as far as identities went. "No."

Jeena leaned back, her other hand against her chin. "I think now is the perfect time for you to ask Keith about it." she said seriously. "And on a side-note, Veren's lucky to have you." she finished, winking at the end.

Brianna blushed, and she stood there, unsure what to say next. "Wait—" she said, her mouth working independently of her brain. "You called me up here to make sure I didn't know, and you won't even tell me what you mean?"

"It's not our place to tell," Skye said simply with a sympathetic smile. "If we did, you'd get mad at Keith for hiding it from you, along with someone else telling you before he did. It's best for you to learn it straight from Keith."

REVELATION

Brianna slowly walked back to Keith's school, acutely aware that she was missing something important: a crucial piece of information about Keith that involved the both of them, and she was completely out of it.

She found Emmy, Veren and James waiting by the front steps of the school building.

"Hey, Bri," Veren greeted, raising a hand as she stepped closer. "We didn't want to start training without you."

"Thanks, Veren," she said faintly, then she breathed in and out. "But you can go ahead and start without me. There's something I gotta talk to Keith about."

They both blinked in surprise, but it was Emmy who spoke up first: "What do you need to talk to Keith about?"

"Something I should apparently know," she said, glancing down. "Something that connects me and Keith together, in a way I don't yet understand. But I intend to find out."

As she said it, there was a change in Emmy and Veren. It was very subtle, but their postures shifted, and the way they were looking at her changed a little. Neither of them answered.

After a few moments, she looked back up. "You guys know too, don't you?" she said, having a feeling of it.

Veren struggled for a moment, then he nodded. "We do," he whispered. "When you were still—asleep, Keith was really devastated, more so than we knew was normal. And when we asked why, we got our answer."

Brianna slowly smiled a bit, nodding. "Okay," she answered. "But don't tell me; I want to find out from Keith himself."

And with that, she stepped past them, walking inside the school.

Emmy watched Brianna walk inside, and once out of earshot, she sighed. "She's frustrated inside," she said, having saw it behind the small smile. "She really wants to know just what we meant and will react based on what Keith says."

"Yeah" Veren murmured, then straightened. "I hope it all goes well when she finds out."

There was a few seconds of silence between them, then James stepped up beside him, head tilted. "Um, would anyone mind telling me what you're talking about?" he asked, raising an eyebrow. "And why can't you tell her? Why must she learn it from Keith?"

Emmy turned toward him. "Bri is Keith's daughter," she said, glancing downward. "That's why she must learn it from Keith."

He blinked several times, surprised. "Whoa—but how? And why didn't she know before now?"

"The *how* we don't know either," she said, sighing. "Bri will learn it, as I suspect she'll have many questions, then tell us eventually. As for *why*, it's a bit of a long story."

James briefly threw up his arms. "I'm all ears."

So she began, while Veren continued to look at the entrance to the school, his expression conflicted.

Brianna walked throughout the school, got instructions from a staff member, and stood in front of Keith's office. Having gotten permission to enter by knocking, she opened the door and stepped inside.

Keith's office was a bit plain, but cozy all the same. The walls, floor and carpet were various shades of light brown. His large wooden desk spanned three-quarters of the room's length, faintly gleaming an amber color from the window's light. Two cabinets sat beside it, one on each side, both dark-brown and fairly stuffed with paperwork. Behind the desk, where Keith sat, was a lit fireplace.

Keith looked up from his current paperwork, then smiled. "Bri," he greeted, his voice warm. "What are you doing here? Aren't you supposed to be training?"

She closed the door behind her, slowly approaching the rightmost chair in front of Keith's desk. "Keith, there's something you're not telling me, isn't there?" she said, slowly sitting down. "Please, I need to know what it is/"

Keith's entire image changed; the warmth was replaced by sadness and weariness, and he seemed to age considerably from it.

He sighed heavily, as if he were barely restrained right then. "Do you remember the day I first met you in the city, three years ago?" he asked, his voice faint.

"Remember? How could I forget?" she answered, that memory flashing before her eyes. She'd been deathly scared of the Oblivion's, much more naive about the world, and considerably more reserved. Keith had saved her, then had essentially given her a perfect offer with no drawbacks or conditions.

He nodded slowly, his gaze fixed on her. "And how I reacted when you told me your name?"

"Yeah," she said slowly, in thought. "You freaked out a little, and I didn't know why. I still don't."

Keith passed a hand over his eyes, but still looked at her. "That's because—" he said, then stopped. "That's because I recognized you, Bri."

She blinked, confused. "Recognized me," she repeated. "Wait, we've met before?"

She racked her brain, but she couldn't ever remember meeting Keith before he saved her. What was going on here?

He nodded, still seeming to struggle for control. "Yes, we have," he answered faintly.

"But," she said, getting a bit frustrated. "But that can't be right. I don't remember meeting you before! When did that even happen?"

"We met before," Keith said, starting to breathe heavily. "Twelve years ago. Wwelve years before I ever saved you"

"You—" she started to say, then it sunk in. Twelve years. That meant he'd been there when she was born, roughly speaking. A shock went through her body, tingling up and down her spine.

Could Keith be . . .

"You were there when I was born?" she whispered, dazed, breathing heavily herself.

Tears started to run down Keith's cheeks, and he looked at her, his eyes full of love, relief, sadness, and pain. "It was my right, as your father," he whispered weakly, the words full of so much emotion.

She gasped, feeling herself grow weak as her intense emotions surged through her body. She felt her eyes grow wet, the first time in a long while.

She tried to stand up, to hug Keith, but her knees wobbled as soon as she tried. She ended up falling to the floor, knocking the chair over.

"Bri!" Keith cried out, almost instantly at her side and pulling her up with a gentle, loving grip. It sent another thrill down her spine.

It all makes sense now, she thought weakly. *I was so stupid not to see it!*

"Keith," she breathed, her vision a little blurry from the tears. "Are you . . . are you really—?" she tried to ask, stumbling.

With his own tears falling slowly, he gave a little smile, and held up his other hand. "Maybe this will help you," he whispered gently, a finger glowing pure white.

Then he gently placed the tip directly on her forehead.

She gasped, a vision forming in her mind's eye. Keith and his office disappeared, and at first, she was in a blank white space. Then tendrils of color splashed onto the scene, weaving across the space before her as she watched, breathing heavily from what she had learned.

Eventually, the scene solidified: she was in the middle of a small field, grass growing neatly all around her. About ten feet away from her was a house built out of stone and wood, with some smoke coming out of the chimney. In the distance, she could see work being done on a stone wall, with workers milling around. She later recognized it as Liark's giant stone wall.

But her attention was focused on the man who stood in front of the house, only five feet away from her: Keith.

He was younger than she had seen five minutes ago, though she couldn't guess how much younger. Still, the amber-brown eyes and brown hair were all perfectly recognizable to her, as was his warm smile. And after her initial glance, she realized he was holding something. She unconsciously stepped closer toward Keith, who gave no indication that he saw or heard her.

Well, this is a memory, she thought faintly, looking down at what Keith was holding. When she did though, she gasped, her heart beating faster.

It was a baby girl, wrapped up snugly in a small white blanket, making cooing noises and waving her little arms around.

Brianna's hand brushed against her mouth, her breathing even heavier. She didn't know how she knew this, but she knew in the deepest part of her heart that the little baby girl was *her*!

"Aw, you're so cute, Bri," Keith whispered lovingly, bouncing the little baby up and down, and chuckling. Her infant self giggled a lot, her little arms flailing.

Then Keith reached into his pocket, pulling something out with a smile. "How do you like this?" he cooed lightly, gently putting it within reach of the baby, who immediately began to grasp and tug at it.

Keith held a chain, attached to which was a figure of a—Fenrir? Brianna looked closer, but something seemed off. It definitely looked wolfish, but it didn't have many of Fenrir's key features.

Maybe it's a normal wolf? Brianna thought slowly, unsure. *"He mentioned one of those once.*

Even as the baby played with the figure, a woman's voice came from inside the house, "Keith! Dinner's ready!"

"Coming!" Keith answered, gently turning and walking into the house with her baby self, leaving Bri standing there, stunned.

And just like that, the memory distorted and faded, reality coming back with a lurch. She gasped, breathing heavily as she got her bearings back, her hand still unconsciously at her mouth. Even as she sat there, she felt the tear stains on her cheeks, both fresh and drying. Her heart beat so much it might have exploded; so great were her emotions.

Keith leaned against his desk, as if he couldn't stand anymore. Fresh tears also lined his cheeks, and he was breathing heavily.

"Keith," she rasped out, then she gasped lightly. "D-dad—"

It all happened so fast. One moment there were apart, barely able to stand; then they were pressed against each other, buried in each other's arms.

Brianna cried fresh tears, trembling as she held onto Keith and feeling herself go weak at the knees. Keith held her so tightly she might have had trouble breathing, but he was trembling too, even as his tears fell onto her clothes.

Outside, Emmy and Veren lightly sparred, stepping it up with every passing minute. James watched from the sidelines, interested but only showing it with a raised eyebrow.

They eventually stopped, panting heavily. Veren wiped at his sweat. "Not bad, Emmy," he said with a smile. "But we can do better."

"We'll need to," Emmy answered, stretching heavily with small grunts. "We can't let ourselves slip up again."

He nodded, then looked around him. "Bri's not back yet," he said, growing concerned. "And it's starting to get late."

Emmy looked up from her leg stretch, then slowly straightened. "These things take time, Veren," she said gently. "Bri will be back when she's ready."

"That doesn't stop the worry," he said, sighing as he looked back at the school.

"Dad," Bri rasped weakly, still holding onto Keith tightly, tears staining his shirt.

They remained that way for what seemed like an eternity, holding each other tightly, tears falling freely. But eventually, Keith pulled apart, just enough for him to look at her, his breathing heavy.

"Oh, Bri," he rasped, his hand going through her hair and his eyes trembling. "I've waited so long, and now you finally know."

"But—" she rasped, breathing heavily, barely able to think with all the intense emotions. She weakly gestured around her, and when she started, she couldn't stop. "How? How did all this happen? I remember living with my family in this little village, that was attacked, then I came here! How did I end up there if I'm your daughter? And why did it happen at all!"

By the end of it, she was out of breath and panting hard, stumbling backward onto the chair.

Keith stepped forward and fell to his knees in front of her. "I don't know all the answers myself, Bri," he breathed, and his tone gained a little desperation. "One night, the house was attacked and I didn't see by who or by what. But you were both gone, and I was devastated."

"That night," she repeated weakly, then she wiped hard at her eyes, as the tears were starting to blur her vision. "Wait, please."

So with both of them breathing heavily, Keith stumbled backward until he held his desk with both hands to support himself. He made no attempt to wipe the tears from his cheeks.

For a few moments, she slowly got her strength back, gaining some control. She still felt her emotions as intensely as before, and she had so many questions, but now she could think and listen effectively. Then she looked up, her eyes still a bit weak, but faintly determined. "That memory you showed me," she whispered a bit weakly, "was that before the attack you mentioned?"

He nodded heavily, his own gaze weak. "Yes, it was," he breathed, briefly closing his eyes. "A full week before it."

"Then what happened?" she asked, getting stronger with every word.

He slumped a bit, but he opened his eyes. "It all started simply enough. I had put you to bed and went to sleep myself. The next morning, I woke up and found the house wrecked, both you and my wife missing, and myself mysteriously unscathed."

"That's-that's awful" Bri said, feeling fresh tears falling. Then she blinked a little. "Wait—your wife?"

"The woman's voice you heard in the memory," he said, smiling a sad little smile, for a moment at least. "My beloved. If you're still alive, maybe she is too."

His voice broke on the last part, and he slumped even further. His body was racked with little sobs, even as he struggled to stop. As he did so, he clutched at a ring on his finger.

She didn't completely understand, but the pain on his face was enough for her. "Dad," she breathed sadly, instantly up and holding onto him tightly again.

One hand weakly hugged her back, but fresh tears continued to fall.

Partly to distract him from his sadness, and partly because she was curious, she looked again at the golden ring on his finger. "You know," she breathed, half-closing her eyes, "I've never seen that ring before today."

He took in a deep shuddering breath, then looked back at her, breathing slowly. "It's my wedding ring, Bri," he said, both sadly and with a touch of fondness. "I-I don't wear it in public, because if someone noticed, and asked where my wife was—well, I couldn't answer them," he rasped at the end. "I myself don't know, and it would be too painful to answer. I don't wish my students to see me like that"

Her eyes grew wet again, and she forcefully shut her eyes, hugging Keith a little tighter. "Dad," she rasped, understanding. "Daddy, you've endured so much"

"And that's not even all of it, Bri," he rasped, his hand on her back. "You remember the intelligence force I have at my command?"

She looked up, her eyes still weak, but she nodded. She remembered Keith mentioning them; and in fact, their indirect help had been key to rescuing Emmy from Setxis.

"Well, not long after you both went missing, I asked for their help," he breathed, more tears streaming down his face. "I paid them—have been paying them all these years—to search the land with their minds for you both. For twelve years, there was no news, and each year I lost a little more hope that you were both alive."

And with that, he openly sobbed into her shoulder, and she clutched him with all her might. She breathed heavily, halfway in shock about this, even as her tears had now dried. He had been searching for her all those years and never once stopped. It made her heart burst with warmth, deeply filling up her entire being.

The same warmth Veren evoked in her: love.

"And to think," he continued weakly, even as her grip tightened. "Six of those years you spent were in this very city, under our noses the entire time. If I had only known—"

"Stop!" she yelled, which sounded much weaker than she expected. "Please, Dad, stop."

She didn't know if it was the fact that she had spoken, or her yell, but he stopped in surprise. "Bri," he breathed, looking at her, still breathing a bit heavily.

"What's done," she said, drawing on her mental strength, her eyes pleading, "is done. So please, don't torture yourself any more, please."

His response was to hug her again, which she fiercely returned.

"I never thought I'd see you again, Bri, until that day," he whispered faintly, but sounding partially like himself again. "And now you're a confident, strong, and loving young woman."

"I'm not that confident," she mumbled a bit.

"And yet I couldn't be more proud of you, Bri," he said lovingly.

Moved, she hugged him tightly for the next few minutes, just wanting to hold him.

And eventually, they pulled apart, having gained their strength back, even if gradually. Keith finally seemed to realize he had tear stains on his cheeks, and absentmindedly wiped at them.

It was then that Bri finally saw that the day had turned into night, as the light had faded considerably. "I—" she said, suddenly feeling a bit awkward. She didn't know what to say now, and she had nothing else to ask, that she could think of right then. "I, uh, I guess I should get to bed. I gotta train hard tomorrow, after all."

He looked at her for a moment, then he smiled slightly, and she saw the Keith she knew in it. "Yeah," he said simply, stepping closer. "Goodnight, Bri," he finished, gently kissing her forehead.

Even with that kiss, she knew Keith's love was entirely different from the love between her and Veren. It was strange, yet seemed completely natural. She smiled back a bit. "Goodnight, Dad," she breathed, hugging him again, but more slowly this time.

But when she reached the door and her hand was on the knob, she paused. "Wait," she said slowly, putting a fist over her heart, partly turning around. "One thing."

Keith simply tilted his head.

"If you knew I was your daughter when you saved me," she whispered, feeling a bit strange, "why didn't you tell me right then?"

He glanced down, then he chuckled lightly, though it wasn't too strong. "Think, Bri," he said, looking up at her. "You had lived in this city for six years, learning to survive and do whatever it took to get things done, without hesitation. If I, a stranger who had just saved your life, told you I was your father—well, would you really have believed me?"

She smiled a bit after a moment. "No," she breathed. "In fact, I probably would have just scoffed at you—and then ditched you as soon as I could."

His smile widened a bit. "A good point," he said gently. "And hard as it was, I knew it would be better to wait, before I told you."

She simply looked at him for a few moments, taking it all in. Keith, the man who had saved her in more ways than one. The man who given her a home again and friends, and had even indirectly introduced her to love; a man who cared for her and raised her as though she was his own daughter.

Well, I was, and he did, she thought, feeling warm again. *My father.* Outside her head, she slowly turned the knob, "Thank you," she whispered softly. "For everything."

TESTED

August 10, 2028

Bri stirred as the sun shone brightly on her eyelids, her eyebrows furrowing from the slight pain. It took her a moment to wake up, but eventually she did, sitting up as the blankets fell around her.

And the first thing that struck her mind was the events of yesterday—finding out that Keith was her father.

She smiled without knowing it, feeling warm just from thinking about her father. Then it hit her. The little necklace she'd gotten her first day here—the one she'd suspected Keith had left there for her—that she hadn't really worn, but never got rid of either. She got out of bed quickly, looking at the small table beside her bed.

There it lay: a simple white necklace with a heart-shaped pendant with the word *love* written in flowing lines on one side. The majority of the time, she'd kept it in her pockets as she was unsure what to do with it.

She took it by the chain, holding it up before her eyes, smiling. Then without hesitation, she put it on over her neck, tucking it underneath her outfit. A very small part of the chain was still visible as she made a final adjustment, then got her hair back to normal.

After getting ready for the day, she walked to the door and opened it, only to stop with a small start. Veren was standing outside, apparently waiting for her.

He raised a hand, smiling softly. "Hey," he said simply. "Have a good sleep?"

"Yeah," she answered, then for the third time in ten minutes, a thought struck her. She made a weak noise, looking down with a blush. "I'm so sorry about yesterday night," she said, not sure how he'd react. "I completely forgot about all of you—"

Which was when Veren hugged her, chuckling a little, much to her blinking surprise.

"I'm not mad," he said gently, pulling apart enough to look at her. "None of us are. We all know what you and Keith were talking about. You just had other things on your mind"

It took her a few moments to respond, and she made a weak giggle. "I'm still sorry," she whispered sheepishly, blushing a little.

"It's no problem, Bri," he said. "Seriously."

She smiled softly, but after a few seconds, she slowly looked down at the way he held her arm. His grip, while not tight, was certainly too close for her comfort.

Veren slowly looked down at this arrangement, then back up at her. She saw the realization flit in his eyes, before he looked back down at their joined arms. Then slowly, he loosened his grip and withdrew a foot, then put his hands behind his back.

"Sorry," he said awkwardly. "I know you don't like it when I cling, but I just— well, what I'm trying to say is—"

She took his hand, which got his attention. "I understand, Veren," she said, hoping she was able to convey all her feelings about this. "You're worried it'll happen again, and I do appreciate that. But I still don't like it when you're restricting me."

He glanced down for a moment. "Restricting," he repeated faintly, then got a small smile. "I guess it makes me look like a fool, huh? But it'll take time before I get over it."

She didn't like that, but she managed a smile as she leaned against Veren. "Well, then," she breathed gently, "I guess it's one day at a time."

She felt his smile, and his kiss against her forehead was warm. She enjoyed that, but she also enjoyed it when her other hand brushed against her father's necklace.

August 16, 2028

For the week, the three of them trained hard every chance they got, even as James watched. They started with the basics, then worked their way up. The first day had been hard on their bodies, as they hadn't done this kind of training for awhile. After that, their previous experience gradually overrode this feeling, even as they continued to push themselves harder.

Brianna breathed heavily as she bent over a bit, slowly taking a moment to wipe the sweat off her forehead. "Okay," she said. "I think we're getting back to our old skill levels."

"Good to know," Veren rasped a little, lightly sitting down to recover. "Of course, we need another break here."

"Of course," she said a bit gently, sitting down close to him.

Emmy sat across them, also recovering, but her eyes curious. "While we're sitting here," she started. "There's something I'd like to know."

"Which is?" Bri asked, looking at her.

"That night, when we faced that thousands-strong Oblivion army," she said, tilting her head, "you saved us, but I think I noticed you holding four different warpblades, two floating—did you have a new drive or something?"

She blinked, and she briefly stared off into space, trying to remember.

It was fairly easy, as though it had been months for her friends, it had merely been weeks for her. It had been a sea of Oblivions, which made her shudder inwardly, and near-endless repetitions of fighting and pain. She'd almost given up but faced the last through force of will. And now that she thought about it, she *had* seemed to have decimated them too easily at the end.

"I *think* I did," she said, sounding unsure. "But it's hazy, and I wasn't really paying attention."

"Well, maybe when we've recovered fully, you can try and see," Emmy said, smiling.

"You always were ahead of us in drives, Bri," Veren said playfully, lightly bumping her shoulder with his, which made her smile.

"Yeah," Emmy agreed with a giggle. "You work just as hard as we do, but you have natural talent helping you."

"You mean, Keith?" she said, a little embarrassed, glancing at Veren. "And you guys aren't that far behind!"

"Thanks for that," Veren answered, taking her hand briefly. "And of course we mean Keith. I believe he said he worked with swords before the world changed, as a hobby."

"Which is exactly where you got your natural talent from." Emmy said, slowly standing up and stretching. "Speaking of which, I think we've recovered enough."

They stood up with her, also stretching from sitting. "So, I should try to see if I have a new drive now?" Bri asked, to which her friends simply nodded.

She breathed slowly, closing her eyes, thinking back to what she felt before her last burst of willpower. A few moments later, she tentatively thought it was the resolve not to let the Oblivions attack the city, or Keith. Other than pain and despair, that was the only notable thing she had felt. But even as she stood there unsure, there was a gasp from her friends.

She snapped her eyes open. "What? What!" she said quickly.

"You have a new drive all right," Emmy said, but it was faint. She looked scared.

"But that can't be it," Veren said, as if saying it made it not true.

She looked down, utterly confused.

Though she held no warpblades just yet, her training outfit had changed—it was now black with dark-blue accents. All she was missing were the yellow eyes.

She gasped and staggered backward, tripping over her own feet, flashing out of the drive in her panic. This staggered her friends out of their shock.

"Bri!" Veren cried out, instantly at her side, and Emmy there shortly afterward.

"That can't be my new drive!" Bri said in a rush, breathing heavily. "It just can't be!"

"It's okay, Bri!" Veren said, quickly drawing her into a hug, holding her tightly. "It's okay, it's okay."

While Emmy held a concerned expression, Veren's hug didn't leave a lot of room for her. She stood up faintly, letting them have their moment while also hearing footsteps.

Turns out, it was James, coming back from getting his lunch. He was currently finishing up an apple.

"Hey, Emmy," he greeted, slightly off because he was still eating. "How's training going—" he trailed off when he saw Bri and Veren together, then he got a confused look. "I missed something, didn't I?"

"Uh," she said, feeling a little awkward as she glanced at them, and not just from the moment they were intruding on, "yeah."

He made a small sound, took the last bite out of his apple, then chucked the core. "It must be hard being a third wheel," he said, looking at her with understanding.

She was surprised, staring at him. "Um, how did you know that?" she asked, glancing toward the thrown apple core, inwardly thinking that was a nice throw.

He sighed, hands in pockets. "Because I'm feeling much the same," he said. "In addition to feeling guilty about everything I've done while brainwashed, I feel like I'm intruding on your friendship by being a fourth wheel."

"Well, you're not intruding," she answered, faintly impressed. "And though I am a third wheel at times, I'm okay with it, as long as I still get to hang out with my friends. And I do."

"I've seen that," James said gently. "But I think I have a knack for seeing what's under the surface."

She looked at James, seriously reevaluating her opinion of him. Veren had been right; James was nothing like Setxis, and there was more to him than her biased eyes had seen.

She had just begun to smile when James's eyes wandered, confused. "What's that sound?"

She listened, looking around. "I don't hear any—" she started, only to trail off.

No she thought in horror.

It was. The air began to fill with a half-hissing, half-sizzling sound, and it wasn't just a few of them. She summoned her warpblade by instinct, while she knew, without looking, that Bri and Veren had scrambled to their feet, also summoning their warpblades.

"Whoa whoa! What's happening?" James asked in slight panic, backing away a step from her weapon.

"Just get inside the school, and stay there," she said tightly. Taking her friend's wrists behind her, she dragged them along. "Come on, we gotta tell Keith! We gotta get a plan here!"

James stared after them, blinking once, then sighed faintly. Then he crossed his arms and craned his neck a little, looking at the fading shape of Emmy's warpblade. "Where do those things come from anyway?" he wondered aloud, bemused as he started to run inside.

Much later, Bri, Emmy, and Veren slowly walked back to Keith's school. They were exhausted, scratched up a little, and just plain sick of Oblivions by now.

"Well, *that* passed by quickly," Veren breathed, trying to sound light, but only half-succeeding.

"Yeah," Emmy breathed, twisting her neck a little to the right, trying to get rid of a kink. "That seemed like, what, five minutes?"

"Probably hours" Bri guessed, wondering how it was that time passed when you didn't want it to and slowed when you did want it to. Still, either way, she didn't want to think about the attack; it all horribly reminded her of what the guards had done many months ago, destruction and injuries included. And by the general demeanor of Veren and Emmy, they didn't want to think about it much either.

"Seemed like five minutes though."

"This can't go on," Keith said tensely. "That's twice in two months that a massive army has popped up, and this one actually attacked our city in broad daylight. Something must be done."

"I agree," Veren said, with an edge in his voice.

Bri took his hand, squeezing it. "But what?" she asked.

Keith opened his mouth to speak, but a man came up to him. "Keith, there's new intelligence on the situation."

"Go on," he said, then in an undertone to the three teenagers, he told them, "Ray, head of the intelligence service I've used."

"Our team was scouring the Hearts Mountains, and they noticed a disturbance at the tallest one," Ray started, looking grim. "Closer examination revealed an army of Oblivions, coming straight down from the tip. Mere seconds after we discovered this fact, they disappeared into the side of the mountain. Unable to locate them again, the team directed their thoughts toward the tip of the tallest mountain. They discovered a person up there—a woman."

"Why hasn't the team discovered her there before?" Keith asked, looking straight at him. "If I recall correctly, searching out with your minds should reveal any living being, even if just a trace."

"She should have been revealed," he said, his tone a bit hard, but it faded. "But it seems this individual had the ability to shield herself from our search. We're speculating that she has been hiding from our scans for years, though we fail to understand how she has done this."

"But you've identified her?" Keith asked

Ray shook his head. "Not precisely," he said. "Other than some aspects of her appearance, and gender, we've been unable to gather more than that. Though we heavily suspect she's letting us scan her now, for some unknown reason."

"Her appearance," Keith said, suddenly intent. "Describe her."

"The woman had blue eyes, and long brown-black hair," Ray said, glancing upward as he recalled. "She wore a dark-purple shirt and red-violet pants. Those were the clearest things we could discern. The rest was too fuzzy to make out."

Keith turned to his right, quickly hiding his reaction from all of them. However, Bri caught a glimpse of it; he had paled a little, and his breathing had become heavier. But why?

And why did she have the slightest feeling that she'd seen that look before?

"Keith?" Emmy asked, tilting her head. "Is something wrong?"

"Uh, no," he said, his voice slightly higher on the first word, turning back to them. "Just my suspicions. I don't know enough to speculate right now though."

"The question still remains. What will we do about this, Keith?" Veren said, squeezing Bri's hand. "It's very likely this woman is directing the Oblivions. And who knows, she may have even created them in the first place!"

"I'm with him, sir," Ray said, nodding, "on the 'something must be done' part."

"Yes, it must," Keith muttered, though only because he held his hand near his mouth, in thought. "But those are some nice theories, Veren. Anyway, Bri, Emmy, Veren, you three will go up that mountain and confront this woman. If possible, bring her back to Liark, preferably alive."

The three teenagers nodded grimly, though Ray tilted his head. "If I may ask, sir," he said, "why them?"

Keith looked back at him with a small smile. "Because, Ray," he answered, "these three are my most skilled students, and they've been ordered by the king and queen themselves to confront the individual responsible anyway. All that's changed is we know exactly where she is."

He was silent for a moment, then nodded. "All right," Ray answered, then turned to the three teenagers. "All that's needed is transportation."

"If I may ask, how will we transport ourselves up there?" Veren asked, his eyebrows furrowed.

"That's already being arranged," he answered, then smiled slightly. "And it's waiting outside."

This made all three of them blink in surprise.

Turns out, their transportation was a Fenrir.

Not *their* Fenrir, to Bri's disappointment, but one of his kind regardless. This one was about ten feet tall, with mainly slate-gray fur, but with quite a lot of black as well. His mane and tail hair seemed more groomed than their Fenrir's, but the fur directly above his paws was much thicker than normal. He regarded them with skeptical dark-gold eyes and was currently stretched out to allow people on his back.

"All right, climb on his back," Ray said, stepping back. "The sooner the better."

"Right," Bri agreed, the first to climb up, Emmy and Veren following shortly afterward. He stood up a second after they finished, leaving them briefly scrambling for a handhold.

"Be safe, Bri," Keith said with a smile, reaching up with his hand.

Bri smiled softly, and shook it with a nod. "You too, Dad," she whispered, feeling a thrill upon saying it.

And with that, the gray Fenrir took off, leaving the three teenagers struggling to hold on. The two men watched them go for awhile.

Then Ray turned toward Keith. "'Dad,' sir?" he asked, an eyebrow raised.

Keith chuckled a bit sheepishly. "I'll fill you in later," he said, smiling a bit, "when things have calmed down."

"But there's another reason why only those three are going, isn't there." he said, his tone indicating that it wasn't a question.

Keith shook his head, his expression grim. "Yeah," he answered, "because personally, I thought sending anyone else would only mean more casualties."

"What makes you think that?" Ray asked, his eyebrows furrowed.

Keith sighed, still looking at the spot where the Fenrir had disappeared from. "It's kinda a law of the universe," he said faintly. "People who are unimportant to the plot are the most likely to die. And Bri, Emmy, and Veren don't fit that mold because they are apparently important to this woman's plot—whatever it is."

Ray made a disgruntled sound, and looked at the spot where the Fenrir had disappeared also. He did not hear Keith's last comment though.

"I just hope that woman isn't who I think she is."

SHADOWS

The gray Fenrir traveled fast, forcing the three teenagers to grip his fur tightly.

He wasn't one to talk much as his opinion of humans wasn't that high. Despite that, he still showed respect to their Fenrir by being friendly enough to them. Bri closed her eyes, slowly reaching for his mind, trying for a tendril connection as Fenrir had done with her. At first she felt nothing, then she was intercepted by this Fenrir's mind.

What? he asked, his tone blank.

She was briefly surprised, but she had to remind herself that this wasn't her Fenrir. *Um, how's your alpha doing?* she thought after a moment, thinking that he might not know which Fenrir she was referring to if she.

He and the rest of the pack are engaged in battle, he responded, with a slight growl across their mental link. *And once I have transported you three, I will rejoin that battle.*

Oblivions, she thought, not really expecting anything else.

Correct, he answered. *But these Oblivions are not like the others.*

Are they stronger and faster? she asked, tilting her head even though he couldn't see that.

Smarter, he growled, *"in more ways than one, and suddenly they will not die when we tear them to shreds.*

What exactly do you mean? she thought, feeling a sinking feeling in her gut. Oblivions were scary enough, now they were gonna get worse?

We rip one apart with a claw and it's slashed in half, then suddenly it reforms, he said, with an offhand growl. *I do not know where they have suddenly gotten this power, but we will find a way to kill them permanently.*

Her stomach sank lower upon hearing that, and she forced herself to take several deep breaths. *Great,* she thought glumly.

A thought struck her, and she nervously gripped his fur a little tighter. *Hey, um, what problem do you have with humans?*

My issue is with your infinite diversity, he said with what seemed to be a scoff. *You're never predictable, and you're always throwing your weight around at others in your way, so let's just say that makes me wary of you humans.*

She had no idea how to respond to that, so she managed a small nervous laugh. *Well, we don't have to like each other to work together,* she thought to him, and received a slight growl in return.

At the same time that Bri was mentally communicating with the gray Fenrir, Emmy and Veren were having their own conversation, though aloud.

"What do you think this woman's like?" Veren asked, looking back at her. "Her personality, I mean."

Emmy hummed in thought for a few seconds. "Well, the most obvious that come to mind are the 'homicidal maniac,' the 'well-intentioned extremist,' the 'complete monster,'—" she said, counting off on her fingers without even looking.

"Whoa whoa!" he said quickly, blinking in surprise. "Where are those coming from?"

She looked at him and giggled a bit. "Sorry about that," she said. "Those are just fancy descriptions of typical villain molds."

"And you know them how?" he asked, tilting his head.

"You remember how my parents are merchants?" she asked. When he nodded, she continued, "Well, because they were never around, I was usually alone at home surrounded by books on the subjects of math. It's why I'm so good with math. But there were a few books that didn't involve numbers."

"Let me guess," he said, briefly stopped by a bump in their journey. "A list of types of villains?"

"More or less," she answered, giggling a bit. "And it came with general descriptions of what that villain was generally like."

"Well, I just hope she isn't any of the three types you mentioned." he said faintly, briefly looking forward. Then he looked back with a grin, "But that reveal still came outta nowhere, Emmy."

"Hey, friends can still surprise each other!" she said, lightly hitting him on the shoulder, then quickly gripping the gray Fenrir's fur again. "And you never asked!"

"Yeah, but still!"

When both conversations ended, the gray Fenrir reached the bottom of the Hearts Mountains. He quickly ascended with practiced ease, but the angle of ascent forced the three teens to grip even tighter. It also made any conversation much harder, so they kept silent during the trip. He eventually stopped on a flat surface jutting from the side, about fifteen feet below the top.

They slowly dropped to the ground, while the gray Fenrir caught his breath. Slowly putting a hand on his fur, she smiled a bit and thought to him, *I know we cause you concern, but we can't thank you enough for helping us.*

He looked at her for several seconds, then he growled slightly, and stood up. They backed up quickly as darkness enveloped him, and he traveled through the shadows.

"Good luck," she said faintly, looking at the spot where he had disappeared.

A hand took hers gently. "It'll be okay, Bri."

She looked up with a small smile. "Thank you, Veren," she whispered, then blinked. Veren had stepped a lot closer. "What?"

He smiled, looking a little nervous. "Well, I think a good-luck kiss might be in order," he said, stammering slightly at the end. "Just in case."

She admitted she didn't know why he was saying this, but it was not like she would turn down a kiss, so she smiled softly. "Well, okay," she said, pulling him closer.

Emmy scratched her head and developed a sudden interest in her fingernails. She waited till the count of five, then she looked up with an amused smile. "If you two are done, we have a woman to confront," she said loudly, startling them badly.

She giggled, then simply started climbing up the small stretch of mountain above her, Bri and Veren following quickly afterward, both slightly pink in the face.

When they got to the top though, they found a very big surprise.

From Liark, the mountain's tip looked just the same as any other. But it was gone.

The entire tip of the peak they were standing on, some hundreds of feet of rock, had been sliced clean through by something, leaving a flat, empty stretch of mountain rock. Above them, unnatural clouds swirled endlessly.

And sitting patiently in the middle of the flat peak was a woman.

"That's her, I presume," Veren said in a low voice, summoning his warpblade and apparently disregarding the flat peak. Bri and Emmy both followed suit, keeping their eyes on her, but Bri was especially wary. This woman must be powerful to have done this.

"Be ready for anything," Emmy warned, her breathing slow.

Brianna took a deep breath. This was it. "Right," she said, and started walking forward. "Come on."

All three walked together, keeping their eyes on the woman and slowing to a stop about five feet away. "Who are you?" Veren asked, his voice tense.

The woman looked up, and as sure as Ray had described, she had blue eyes, long brown-black hair, a dark-purple shirt and red-violet pants. But that wasn't the complete description of her appearance. She had a black belt wrapped around her waist, with a blue diamond in the middle. She wore brown stockings that stopped just short of her pants, and she wore white sneakers, which had hints of dark-green stains.

She smiled from her seat, completely confident. "My name is Claire," she said. "And you must be Brianna, Emmy, and Veren."

"How do you know about us?" Emmy demanded. Bri had the strangest feeling that Claire's voice sounded familiar. But she shook it off. Now wasn't the time for that.

Claire tilted her head, legs crossed. "It isn't that hard to keep tabs on the city from here, you know," she said, smiling. "Or hide myself from anyone who might wish to find me. I've had a lot of practice on both matters, even before they started looking for me."

"Okay, whatever," Bri said, feeling that there were more pressing questions. "Do you control the Oblivions?"

"Yes," she said simply, like it was obvious. "And I created them, though the initial creation wasn't easy."

The frank answer baffled her. *Why is she just admitting everything?* "Well, that's horrible!" she cried without thinking. "Do you have any idea what those monsters have done to the world?"

"Cause terror, and mayhem," she said, brushing a few hairs out of her eyes. "But if you looked closely, there were very few deaths. Mostly I've been using them to build up your skills and instincts."

"What?" Emmy muttered in complete disbelief. "Why on earth would you do that?"

"And you can't call the death of my village just a few!" Bri cried out, breathing heavily. "Do you have any idea what I've been through?"

Claire got a pained expression, and she sighed, running a hand along her temple. "That was an unfortunate, terrible accident," she said, sounding genuinely pained as well. "The Oblivions had been growing restless, and some were rebelling, so a few slipped away from me. By the time I got them back under control, you were the only one left alive"

Bri's hands clenched hard, and she found herself unable to speak. This woman, even if by accident, was the reason everything had happened to her—

Claire looked up, and her tone lightened. "But on the bright side, if that hadn't happened, you might never have met Emmy and Veren."

Brianna had already opened her mouth to yell something, but even in her anger, the words hit home. It was true, she might never have met them otherwise. Her emotions became so conflicted that her vision briefly blurred with tears.

She struggled for a few seconds, then she found her voice. "Is that supposed to be funny?"

"Why would it be funny?" Claire asked, blinking, looking and sounding confused.

This also baffled her, but it didn't stop her heavy breathing. Even through her anger, she thought this woman was nothing like she'd expected.

"All right, I've heard enough," Veren muttered, and walked forward, aiming his sword at Claire's neck. "We're here, Claire, to confront you and take you back to Liark, by force if necessary."

Bri felt worry worm its way through her anger, and she looked at Emmy, who sighed a bit. "He's feeling pained because of how upset you are," Emmy said in an undertone.

Meanwhile, Claire glanced at the warpblade without fear, even though it was mere inches away from her neck. "Well, perhaps I would come along after the fighting," she said, smiling as she looked back up at him. "I do enjoy the fighting aspect."

Veren blinked slowly, staring at her, confused.

Claire chuckled, uncrossing her legs and standing up, which jolted Veren and kept his sword at her neck. "You know, you can't keep that blade at my throat forever," she said, looking down at him slightly, as she was taller than Veren. "Not if we're gonna fight. And to be fair, I'd like it to be three-on-one, with no drives"

"Fair," he repeated slowly, blinking. "How is that fair?"

"I think you'll find out," she answered simply, smiling. "And what fun would it be to start off with the high level stuff?"

Then she held out her left hand.

Out of thin air, she summoned a warpblade, much to their surprise. The blade was colored blue and gleamed despite the poor lighting. The guard was a dark golden color while the handle was pitch-black. The diamond shapes were a very cloudy shade of silver.

Veren backed up quickly, taking a ready stance, while Bri and Emmy were near-instantly at his side.

"This is gonna be fun," Claire whispered gleefully, taking up her own stance. Then she disappeared in a flash of light.

It all happened in a blur. Claire reappeared above them, slashing in a wide arc. Veren deflected it while Bri and Emmy jumped backward, then pushed her back and pressed the attack. Both women came charging in from different directions, intending to overpower her. Claire waited till the last moment, then quickly dropped herself to one knee.

The result was three warpblades clashing against one another, and the awkward arrangement threw them off balance. Claire skillfully removed herself from underneath their struggle, holding herself in a loose, battle-ready pose a few feet away, but not taking advantage of their moment.

She's good, Bri thought. *I'll give her that.*

So she teleported, coming in from above and behind her, aiming for her shoulder. Claire blocked it without really trying then easily moved around Emmy's stabs, and kicked Veren's thigh, sending his slash awry. There was a brief moment where nothing happened, then the battle resumed.

Minutes passed as the four of them battled, but no one got anywhere. Claire didn't attack them much, and when she did, it was either with moves they could easily block; otherwise, she merely bruised them with the flat part of her warpblade. She never touched them with slashes or stabs, but not because she couldn't do it. The three of them simply couldn't overpower Claire's technical skill, even with all their experience—years and years of practiced motions and forms.

She was just toying with them. And it turned out, she really was enjoying the combat—there wasn't anything else that could describe the glee in her expression.

Eventually, the three of them stood a small distance away, ready for an attack but breathing heavily. Claire watched them, but made no move.

She's too good! Bri thought, frustrated. *We can't win like this!*

Her hand began glowing red-orange as she prepared to use magic. *So, we'll just have to change things up.*

With a yell, she sent a hail of fireballs at Claire.

Claire didn't move as five of the six fireballs rocketed past her, even when one was inches from her face. Humming to herself, she leaned her head to the right, avoiding the last one by an inch. Acting as though nothing happened, Claire leaned back to her normal position, grinning as if she was having the time of her life.

Bri grunted, even as she ignored the mental drain. *Okay then,* she thought, her hand glowing red-orange again.

"Playing with magic now?" Claire asked, holding up her right hand, which began to glow yellow. "I'm in."

Her senses tingled, but not for her sake; the clouds were darkening over her friends. "Look out!"

Emmy dodged in the nick of time, but the lightning bolts followed after Veren in large arcs. In slow motion, he seemed to see it coming for him, then he swung his warpblade with a wild cry. And at the exact moment, his warpblade connected with them. And he split each one in half, dissipating the lightning bolts completely.

That—that shouldn't have been possible.

Veren stared at the air in front of him, completely stunned. "How?" he asked, only to stop and turn toward them. "How the hell did I just do that!"

"I'd make a crack about once-in-a-lifetime chances, but I think that's what just happened," Emmy said faintly, as though she couldn't believe it herself.

Bri felt much the same, in addition to a dash of 'That was awesome!'—but she had to push it aside. She quickly focused on Claire, who was merely intrigued by what had happened. She clenched her glowing hand and pointed it at her, fire-whips shooting out of her hand, moving fast. Claire saw it coming, and lifted up her warpblade to strike—

A blast of wind disrupted her attempt, and Bri's fire-whips wrapped around her. Bri gave Emmy a grateful look. Thanks to her careful focus, neither she nor Claire were burned or feeling the heat from the fire.

Claire chuckled, smiling. "Not bad," she said, then teleported out of her fiery grip, moving two feet to the left. "Keep it coming, you three. I'm thoroughly enjoying this."

She jumped to the side, dodging Veren's icy magic. She continued to run without concern and sparring with Bri and Emmy, who were trying to stop her. Eventually, Veren focused his second ice magic into a perfect ball, outside his hand. With a shout, he threw it at the ground Claire would run over.

Claire, though, deflected it with the flat of her blade, leaving it intact, and heading straight for Emmy—at which point their reactions quickly turned to horror.

There was a blinding flash of light, then when they finally got their senses back, they stared. A thick ice dome had been set—with Emmy in the middle of it. There was space between her and the ice, judging by the movements, but it was a close call. And when Emmy banged on the ice, shouting something they couldn't hear, she recoiled as small bits of frostbite clung to her fingers.

"Emmy!" Bri cried, running past Claire, who simply stood there. She was just about to pound at the ice in an attempt to help, but was forcefully stopped by Veren.

"Don't do it!" he cried out, holding her by the wrists. "You'll only get hurt. It's too cold to touch directly."

"Then how do we get her out of there?" she asked, really worried.

A warm red light came from the ice, getting their attention—it was coming from inside the ice dome, and Emmy's shadow had vanished. The warm light intensified, nearly blinding them as they quickly stepped away, shielding themselves. Then it did blind them, and a crystalline sound echoed as the ice shattered.

Bri yelped slightly from being pelted by ice fragments, and because she couldn't see, she didn't see Veren doing the same. Thankfully, the larger pieces missed them.

They looked back after a second and saw Emmy standing there, smoke curling off herself but otherwise unaffected.

"Emmy can get herself out," Emmy said with a grin, twirling her warpblade.

She was surprised, but pleased. "But how did you do that?" she said, quickly giving her friend a hug.

Emmy smiled, both from surprise and from the hug, then she giggled. "I simply calculated how much heat I'd need to melt that ice, adjusted for thickness, then gave it my best shot," she said, as if it was an everyday occurrence. Then her mouth twisted slightly, "Though it turns out, I used way too much heat. Oh well."

They heard a hum, and they quickly snapped around. They'd forgotten Claire was right there.

She smiled, tilting her head. "Not bad, not bad at all," she said genuinely. "You three quite clearly know your stuff, as befits three teenagers who have been training for most of the past few years."

"You've been spying on us, haven't you!" Veren yelled, breathing heavily.

"Well," she said, glancing upward in thought. "Indirectly, yes," she responded. "I did watch one or two of your training sessions myself from afar, but for the most part, the ones who've been watching you were the group of guards you know so well."

"*You*" Emmy growled, with such pure hatred her friends had painful flashbacks. "Oh, when I'm through with you, you're gonna be in pieces!"

With a yell, she rushed at Claire, but was barely restrained by Bri and Veren.

"How could you do that!" Bri yelled, wanting nothing more than to let Emmy loose. "Do you know what horrible things they've done?"

"You mean the horrible things I wanted you to think they've done?"

This didn't stop Emmy's struggling, but it did make the rest of them stare at her. "You—what?" she breathed, not understanding.

"Mind control is not just control, you know," she answered instead, rubbing her head. "It can extend to simple little touches, enhancing the feelings that are already there."

Veren glanced at the still-struggling Emmy, putting the pieces together. "You screwed with Emmy's head, didn't you!" he yelled, his grip loosening.

"I thought it'd be fun to watch her go berserk on Setxis," Claire said, then she chuckled. "And it was. But for the most part, your friend didn't need much enhancing."

Veren almost let go of Emmy, but the moment she tried to tear free, he instinctively held her back. Bri was glad he did; as much as she wanted to let Emmy loose, she *hated* seeing her like this.

"And in addition, I can plant fake memories, like I did with the guards you're familiar with," she continued, then she shuddered, looking troubled. "And that was not pleasant, making up those gruesome and disturbing memories."

Emmy didn't seem to hear much of this, as she was still struggling and yelling. Veren looked back at Claire, breathing heavily. "And let me guess, Setxis too?" he said grimly.

"Yeah," Claire said, though she sounded a little pained at his name. "Though it wasn't meant to be that way. My little mind control wasn't supposed to change him completely, but I hit a few snags in the process. And he rendered all my attempts to reverse it null, plus asked for an anti-aging effect. He was quite persistent about it."

Bri's mind flashed back to their infiltration of the guards' headquarters. She had heard mention of an anti-aging thing, but hadn't thought much of it. But now that she thought about it, Setxis hadn't changed much between when she'd first arrived and the time when Emmy had brutally beaten him—more than six years difference.

"How old is James?" she asked suspiciously, her voice a little strained because of the still-struggling Emmy.

"He turned eighteen shortly before you arrived in Liark," Claire said simply, looking at her. "And my anti-aging spell didn't wear off until Emmy electrocuted him, reversing what I'd done. So that makes James twenty-six, technically, but his body is still only eighteen."

This, of all things, struck Emmy speechless. She stopped her struggling, much to her friends' surprise, in addition to the main surprise of James technically being twenty-six.

They were further surprised when a swirling black vortex opened up ten feet to their right. Claire didn't seem surprised, and only smiled as a blur jumped out of it, landing with a thud and a growl.

"Fenrir?" Bri breathed, still too deep in surprise to feel happy to see him, letting go of Emmy. "I thought you were busy."

He glanced at them, and they were jolted slightly as he projected his thoughts to them. *I was,* he answered. *But the Oblivions have suddenly lost their ability to regenerate, and did not come back. However, I traced their owner's scent, and came here.*

"Wait—" Veren said, slowly letting go of Emmy, then glared at Claire. "You."

She glanced back at him, smiling. "Well, I thought giving them something extra might make them a threat again," she said. "Do you know how many you've destroyed? The only reason they're still scary is because of the element of surprise, but that's pushing it sometimes."

A blast of darkness swept through the spot where she'd been standing: Fenrir had attacked, and she had dodged with some surprise, but not with any real effort.

Enough talk! he snarled with his thoughts. His claws began glowing—wait, red-orange!

A ring of fire erupted around Claire, who moved to the center but kept an eye on Fenrir. This took all of two seconds, during which the fire abruptly cut itself off.

Fenrir growled, and it could only have been in frustration; he had clearly not cut it off himself.

He rushed forward, jumping and raising a claw. Claire slipped away from it easily.

Clang!

Claire looked to her right, the clang having been her accidental block from Bri's attack. Her clothes were green with brown accents—her quick drive.

She hummed, grinning. "Now things will get interesting," she whispered with glee, then her own clothes flashed briefly.

Bri stared, both surprised and horrified: Claire's clothes were now black with dark-blue accents—the new drive she herself had gained!

"No!" she gasped, staggering back in fear, her heart beating like crazy. "You can't have gotten that!"

Just looking at that drive brought terrifying flashbacks.

Claire glanced down at herself, and when she looked back up, her expression was actually sympathetic. "I'm really sorry about this, Bri—" she said genuinely. She was about to say more, but Fenrir had resumed his attack, this time with a short-duration burst of icicles.

Brianna stood there, still frozen from the painful flashbacks Claire's drive was giving her. That was until Fenrir's attack cracked the mountain itself, throwing several large stones everywhere, including a few that were bigger than her head.

One of which was coming straight toward her, she realized too late.

A fierce blast of wind struck the rock, blowing it to her left while she was whipped indirectly.

Veren stepped near her, in his resistance drive, breathing heavily. "No one's hurting you," he said heavily.

"Look out!" she yelled; another *slightly* smaller rock headed straight toward them.

Veren looked back just in time, then moved instinctively, bracing himself.

The rock shattered into dust upon impact with his chest, provoking a few coughs from the two of them.

"Of course he'd try something stupid," Emmy said ruefully, waving her hand to clear the air, having just recently gotten there. "People do crazy things when they're in love."

Bri would have responded to that, but she was too worried about Veren: "Are you okay?"

Veren turned toward them slowly, his expression dazed and his walk a little unsteady. "I'm fine," he said faintly, then he wobbled, one hand gingerly touching his chest. "Just remind me to—never to do that again."

He wobbled again, and Bri caught him, Veren briefly flashing out of his drive. Emmy shook her head, looking at Bri, "You take care of Veren," she said. "I'll help Fenrir, and you two can join in whenever."

Emmy ran forward, while Bri lightly shook Veren, who was still a bit unsteady. "Veren, come on," she said, holding him upright. "You're gonna be okay."

"Yeah, as soon as my vision clears up," he said, tilting rather dangerously.

"Uh—" she breathed, trying to think of what else to say or do. She needed something to jolt him through this.

She brought him up, and kissed him full on the mouth.

He jerked from surprise, and the sound he made was heavily muffled. She withdrew after that moment, and they both just stared at each other, each surprised at what just happened.

"Uh, thanks, Bri," he said, a little pink from surprise, quickly standing up by himself now. "Just warn me next time, okay?"

"I'll try," she said, also a little embarrassed that she hadn't even hesitated to do that despite the situation being serious. "But right now, there's more important things."

As she said it, her clothes flashed, turning her clothes green with brown accents again.

He nodded quickly, then the same process happened with him, though his clothes turned maroon with black accents: his courage drive.

They both rushed forward into the battle, though Bri traveled much faster, almost looking like streaks of light.

Bri saw much of the battle in slow motion, because she was simply going much faster than everyone else. Well, *almost* everyone else. Clearly the new drive Claire possessed (and the one she herself had gotten earlier) was fast, but not quite up to the quick drive's extent. This gave Claire enough of a warning to see her coming, though she did manage to get a few hits in.

And whenever they didn't teleport out of her vision, Emmy and Veren were doing their part to try to stop Claire. Veren jumped some truly insane distances into the air and always keep his combos going, forcing Claire to keep her defense up. Emmy threw a lot of magic at Claire, further forcing Claire to defend herself. She ran out eventually, but after that, she resorted to the drive's rapid-fire bullets. The air was filled with the constant flashes of light, though many were brief.

Bri slashed at Claire, who teleported, while Emmy jumped off Veren's warpblades and kept her busy with bullets. Landing on the ground with Veren following shortly after, Bri looked up and quickly spotted Claire again. "I'm gonna surprise her from above," she said quickly. "When she's distracted, get her."

And with that, she teleported at least a hundred feet in the air, then reoriented herself. Giving a yell, she drew back her hands for a two-handed strike.

Claire saw her coming, of course, and their warpblades met with a resounding clang. Veren made his move though, swinging himself at Claire, who defended herself mentally with her remaining two warpblades. Claire simply laughed, but only because she was having so much fun. Because of this, she failed to spot the magic forming directly below them.

With a jolt, all three of them were forcefully pulled downward in different directions. Bri and Veren teleported themselves downward, much like Emmy had done.

Claire tried to get her bearings back, but Bri and Veren didn't let her, by constantly blasting wind in her face. She managed to make a safe landing though.

At that exact moment, the entire mountain floor they were standing on turned black, and an ominous hissing emanated from it. Off to the side, completely unaffected, stood Fenrir, his claws glowing a purple black.

Everyone else stiffened involuntarily, including Claire. Their bodies jerked, then suddenly, every single body function slowed down.

Bri's vision darkened, then she blacked out.

RETURN

Bri groaned a bit, but only because her muscles were a little sore from use. She slowly opened her eyes, and though it took her a few moments, everything came back to her and she staggered up, ready for a fight. She clutched at her head suddenly, which was the magic-induced headache she'd gotten from fighting.

But it was completely quiet. And she quickly realized Emmy and Veren were unconscious beside her.

But they weren't beside me when I fell unconscious, she thought, a little confused, but kneeling down anyway. It took her a few seconds, but they came around with a similar reaction to her own seconds ago.

They both looked around, then Emmy blinked. "Hey, look over there," she said, pointing.

Claire lay face-up in the center of the mountain, apparently unconscious, with Fenrir standing over her. He seemed to have a claw touching her head, but other than that, it was hard to make out exactly what he was doing.

"Come on," Veren said, quickly standing up, though he did wobble. He hadn't completely recovered from the hit he'd taken to the chest.

"Here" she whispered gently, pulling his arm over her shoulder, supporting him. He gave her a grateful smile, which made her blush, though she made sure they started walking forward.

As they got closer, they saw Fenrir's one claw was glowing a purple black. Fenrir glanced over at them, but he didn't keep his eyes off his work for long.

"What are you doing, Fenrir?" Bri asked, worried.

Keeping this woman unconscious for some time, he projected with his thoughts, to their brief surprise. *My first instinct was to kill her, but I'm aware you humans like to have people pay for their crimes.*

"That's right," Emmy said, then she furrowed her eyebrows. "But one question. Why did your magic knock us unconscious along with Claire?"

Fenrir growled a bit, but it was faint. *I regret having to do that, but I could not take chances,* he thought to them. *This woman is like a snake—slippery to get hold of and with quite a bite. I could not risk only targeting her and having her escape its area of influence.*

"Well, we understand that," Veren said, standing up straight. "Next time though, if you can, a little warning, please?"

I will try, that much I can do, he thought, removing his claw from Claire's forehead.

"Thanks," Bri said, then looked down at the unconscious Claire. "Who is she?" she said, wanting to know now, briefly seeing a ring glitter on a finger of her left hand. "And what did she want with us?"

"I don't know," Emmy said, crossing her arms. "She said she arranged all of this, years of it, just so she could fight us. But I have a hard time believing that," she continued, with a small scoff at the end. "She's messed up our lives and spent years up here—all for a fight?"

"She did look like she was enjoying it, though," Veren said, deep in thought. "That wasn't just joy in her expression, that was something else. Like the very feelings of fighting simply filled her up to her very core, and she was content with that."

Bri looked up at him and glanced at his hand. "You mean—like love?" she said hesitantly, but softly.

Veren looked at her, a little surprised, but nodding faintly. "Yes, exactly like that," he said after a moment, taking her hand.

"One thing's for sure," Emmy said, shaking her head a little. "This woman's not normal, if that's really the only reason she did all of this."

Well, if you take her back to the city, you might get answers out of her, Fenrir projected, getting down on his paws. *As long as you make the proper restraints.*

"Oh, if I know Keith, he's gonna," Veren said, slowly bending down along with Bri. "If anyone messes with the people he loves, they're bound to answer to him."

Together, the both of them easily lifted up Claire, whose head lolled a bit as they moved to a standing-up position. Then they turned, walking Claire over to Fenrir, who was waiting to take them back.

Back at Keith's school, nothing had really changed, except the two people who were impatiently waiting.

A dark vortex swirled into existence, directly in front of them, much to their brief surprise. After Fenrir and the others popped up, they came forward quickly.

"What happened?" Keith asked quickly, his expression slightly confused as to why Fenrir was there.

"We found her, fought her, and knocked her out," Veren said bluntly, "then came back here."

"The middle two with Fenrir's help," Emmy said, then she moved aside a bit, revealing Claire to Keith's line-of-sight.

"What do we do now, Dad?" Bri asked.

He didn't seem to have heard her. He had turned bone-white upon seeing Claire. "No," he breathed, as if it couldn't be true. And immediately after he said it, he rushed forward, roughly pushing Brianna aside without noticing he'd done so.

"Oh!" she breathed, a little surprised and hurt. "Dad, why'd you do that?"

He didn't answer. He was down on his knees, staring intently and disbelievingly at Claire, almost on the verge of breaking down, though they couldn't understand why. "Claire," he breathed, breathing heavily as one hand touched her hair. "Oh why?"

"Dad?" Bri said, now really worried. "What's wrong?"

Keith picked Claire up, slinging her over his back, not answering Bri again. Instead, he start walking toward the gate, his expression extremely conflicted.

The others just stared after him, completely concerned.

Keith walked through the city, moving toward the centerpiece, where Skye and Jeena lived. He was breathing heavily from the long walk and Claire's weight on his back, but he bore it without complaint.

His brain was reeling. He wanted to do so much right now; he wanted to question her, to find out what happened, and why things had happened the way they did.

But he couldn't. If he did so now, she might escape, and he might never see her again. So, painful as it was, he was doing the right thing and putting her in jail.

Please forgive me, Claire, he thought, looking at her lolling head. She did not respond.

Immediately after he thought this, an Oathkeeper blocked his path, ready to restrain him should he force his way through.

Business? it said with no tone at all.

Keith blinked, completely caught off-guard. Now these things could talk? *That's certainly new,* he thought grimly after a moment.

"I need to see the king and queen, immediately," he said aloud. "It's an emergency and a grave matter."

It regarded him for several seconds, and Keith guessed it was communicating with someone else. Then it jerked its claw, gesturing for him to follow.

He did, only slightly slower than the Oathkeeper, which was moving at full speed. It took him less than a minute to get inside, and the Oathkeepers inside the room immediately kept a close watch on him.

"Keith," Skye said, surprised, but grinning all the same as he approached. "What a pleasant surprise."

"No time, Skye," he said curtly, stopping a few feet away. "We've found the one responsible for the Oblivion attacks on this city and also the one who created them."

"If I'm correct, you're referring to the woman slung over your back," Jeena said as she stood up.

"You are," he breathed. "And when she wakes up, she could escape at any time," he continued, the words getting more painful. "She must be put in prison, immediately, with special restraints."

"Already on it," Skye said grimly, gesturing to the nearby Oathkeepers.

Some time later, Bri sat on the steps of her father's school, weary and confused. Emmy and Veren sat beside her, while Fenrir lay stretched at the bottom of the steps, breathing a low growl every now and then. James was standing between them, having been brought up to speed.

And he was furious, to put it mildly. "When I get my hands on that woman, there will be nothing left of her!" he yelled, still pacing.

"Get in line, James," Bri said faintly, glancing down. "She ruined my life first."

Emmy and Veren stared at her, and even James looked at her. Fenrir merely glanced at her, but his pupils were narrowed.

"Bri, I know you're upset," Veren said after a moment, pulling her closer and looking worried. "I understand that, as I'm mad at Claire for what she's done to you."

"I know, but still," she breathed. "I'm just so conflicted here. This woman ruined my life, yet she's not a monster and regrets part of what she's done. I don't know how to respond to that."

"Keep in mind, she could be lying," Emmy said grimly.

Bri sighed a bit, slowly leaning her head against Veren's shoulder. "And I don't think I've felt this angry since Setxis nearly assaulted Emmy."

Emmy looked distinctly uncomfortable, glancing down at her fingers as they played.

James must have felt uncomfortable too, as he quickly changed the subject. "I just can't believe I'm really twenty-six," he said in an odd tone. "Sure, my body's eighteen, and I feel like that, but it's really something."

"Well, you did strike me as an older man," Emmy said faintly, with a definitely playful twist on *older man*.

James looked at her, raising an eyebrow. "Well, at first glance, you'd appear to be just another dumb blonde," he replied mildly.

Bri lifted her head a little, looking at both of them. "Is this what you meant before?" she asked, glancing at Veren. "About them going back-and-forth being common?"

He smiled, nodding as he glanced at them. "Yeah, it's kinda their way of showing friendship," he said, chuckling a little. "James is a natural, and Emmy has finally found a rival to match her snarks, so she enjoys it as well."

She giggled a little, smiling faintly. "That definitely makes me feel a little better," she said, knowing full well Emmy could still hate his guts, all things considered.

You humans are so unusual, Fenrir projected with his thoughts, sounding amused. *All these different ways you can show affection and hatred, among other things.*

Bri looked up, still smiling. "Speaking of different," she whispered, tilting her head, "what happened back on the mountain? How could you suddenly use elements other than darkness?"

It appeared to start when you fell into your coma, he said, with difficulty on the last word. *I had simply sneezed, then smoke curled out of my nostrils. Much later, Veren had the idea that I might have a rare and unique gift that not many others would have.*

Veren nodded, in response to Bri's look. "Yeah, it was something we discussed," he said faintly, rubbing his head. "Though I was massively wishing you were wide-awake at the time."

After that, after much time and practice, I discovered some new powers, Fenrir continued, shaking his fur once. *It turns out, I have access to all the other elements, but only in a limited fashion. I do not have the full measure of my abilities yet, or if it has any costs, but I will learn.*

Bri smiled, looking down at him, but only because she was sitting above him. "Well, that's great news—" she said, only to trail off.

She had noticed something: Keith was walking toward them.

He walked aimlessly, as if he didn't even notice where he was going. His expression made him look older than he was, and his eyes showed so many overlapping emotions, making it difficult to tell what he was feeling.

"Dad?" Bri breathed, slowly standing up. "Are you okay?"

He did not respond or even appear to notice anything. And he kept walking until he disappeared into the school.

They stared after him, and Bri made an angry, frustrated sound. "That's it. I'm gonna find out what's wrong with him," she said firmly, yanking herself away from Veren.

He followed anyway, as did Emmy. "We're right beside you," he said, not offended at all.

Meanwhile, Emmy looked back at James. "This might not concern you, James," she said, without sugar-coating it.

"Anything that concerns my friends concerns me," he said simply, walking past her and jolting Emmy. She stopped for a moment as she watched his back, faintly impressed—then hurried to catch up.

Meanwhile, Fenrir made himself comfortable, considering he couldn't fit through the door. *I'll just wait here,* he thought wryly to himself, knowing whatever they were about to find out was important and that he'd learn in due time.

They found Keith easily. He was sitting in his office, leaning against the wall, his face buried in one hand.

He looked up slowly, his gaze turning to them. His eyes were red, but he put up a small smile. "Hey," he said faintly. "What can I do for you four?"

It was a feeble effort, and they all saw right through it.

"Dad, what happened back there?" Bri said, stepping close. "Please, tell us!"

He glanced away a little, sighing faintly. "Nothing, really," he said heavily, as though he didn't believe it either. "I took Claire to prison, and that's it."

"But there's more to it, Dad!" Bri said, desperate. "We know there is!"

"Wait, wait, wait a minute." Emmy said, her eyebrows furrowed. "How do you know her name, Keith?"

He looked at her, but didn't answer.

"We never said her name when we got back," Emmy continued slowly.

Veren briefly glanced upward in thought, then he looked at Keith. "It's true" he said to all of them. "And when he rushed toward her, I heard him whisper her name."

Bri looked at them as they spoke, then back at her father, feeling desperate and confused now. "How did you know her name, Dad?" she asked faintly.

He sighed, almost visibly deflating. "I know her name because I've met her before," he said heavily. "She's your mother, Bri."

The story concludes in Book 3

Enlightenment

Ultima

CPSIA information can be obtained at www.ICGtesting.com
Printed in the USA
LVOW12s1054240615

443668LV00002B/141/P